In *Forever Spring*, visit with characters first introduced in the highly acclaimed Desire Trilogy by Joan Hohl.

"Why are you shying away from me, Karen?" Paul asked in a voice so soft it felt like a caress.

Her head jerked up. "I'm not!" she said much too forcefully, her lips burning with the memory of his brief kiss.

Paul's dark eyes met her gaze. "Yes, you are," he said. "And I think I know why."

She was suddenly hot and cold and breathless. Wanting to jump up and run but unable to move, Karen moved her head slowly back and forth. She bit her lip to keep from crying out when his hand tightened around hers.

"You know why, too."

"No." Her voice was raspy, whispery, fearful. She didn't want to hear it, didn't want her feelings, her *needs*, put into words....

Dear Reader,

Sophisticated but sensitive, savvy yet unabashedly sentimental—that's today's woman, today's romance reader—you! And Silhouette Special Editions are written expressly to reward your quest for substantial, emotionally involving love stories.

So take a leisurely stroll under the cover's lavender arch into a garden of romantic delights. Pick and choose among titles if you must—we hope you'll soon equate all six Special Editions each month with consistently gratifying romantic reading.

Watch for sparkling new stories from your Silhouette favorites—Nora Roberts, Tracy Sinclair, Ginna Gray, Lindsay McKenna, Curtiss Ann Matlock, among others—along with some exciting newcomers to Silhouette, such as Karen Keast and Patricia Coughlin. Be on the lookout, too, for the new Silhouette Classics, a distinctive collection of bestselling Special Editions and Silhouette Intimate Moments now brought back to the stands—two each month—by popular demand.

On behalf of all the authors and editors of Special Editions,
Warmest wishes,

Leslie Kazanjian
Senior Editor

JOAN HOHL
Forever Spring

Silhouette Special Edition

Published by Silhouette Books New York

America's Publisher of Contemporary Romance

SILHOUETTE BOOKS
300 East 42nd St., New York, N.Y. 10017

ISBN: 0-373-09444-2

First Silhouette Books printing March 1988

Books by Joan Hohl

Silhouette Special Edition

Thorne's Way #54
Forever Spring #444

Silhouette Intimate Moments

Moments Harsh, Moments Gentle #35

Silhouette Romance

A Taste for Rich Things #334
Someone Waiting #358
The Scent of Lilacs #376

Silhouette Desire

A Much Needed Holiday #247
*Texas Gold #294
*California Copper #312
*Nevada Silver #330
Lady Ice #354
One Tough Hombre #372
Falcon's Flight #390

*Desire trilogy

JOAN HOHL,

a Gemini and an inveterate daydreamer, says she always has her head in the clouds. An avid reader all her life, she discovered romances about ten years ago. "And as soon as I read one," she confesses, "I was hooked." Now an extremely prolific author, she is thrilled to be getting paid for doing exactly what she loves best. Joan also writes under the pseudonym Amii Lorin.

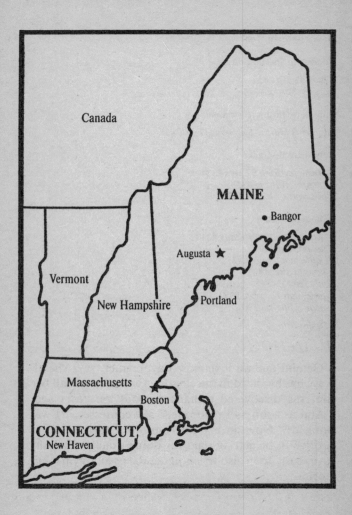

Chapter One

"What a helluva time to start over."

"I beg your pardon?"

Paul Vanzant glanced around sharply at the sound of the soft inquiry. "What?" He frowned at the woman staring up at him. She was seated in a protected niche in the rocks, her arms clasped around her drawn-up knees.

"I said, I beg your pardon," the woman repeated, watching him as he plodded through the sand to her. "Since I'm the only other person on the beach," she said, flicking one hand to indicate the deserted shoreline, "I assumed you were speaking to me."

"I'm sorry." A rueful smile curved Paul's lips. "I hadn't realized I was speaking aloud." He came to a halt a few feet before her and lifted his shoulders in a resigned shrug. "I find myself doing that a lot lately."

"Understandable." The woman's smile was faint.

"It is?" Paul's tone was mildly questioning; his glance was intent, comprehensive. Even though she was seated, he could tell the woman was rather tall. Her figure was full, rounded, not overblown but not svelte, either. She was not beautiful in the accepted sense; her features were too strong, too well-defined. But she was attractive, and her hair was a thick, gorgeous mass of chestnut waves, now blowing freely in the brisk breeze. "Why is it understandable?" he asked, smiling easily.

"I do it myself," she responded, returning his smile and leaving him breathless. "Ever since the season ended I've caught myself muttering my thoughts aloud." Releasing her grip on her knees, she raised one arm. "Would you give me a hand up?"

"Certainly." Intrigued, Paul grasped her hand and drew her to her feet, which were, he noted, encased in expensive but battered-looking running shoes. "Why since the season ended?" he asked when she was standing beside him.

"I've been pretty much alone since then," she explained absently, brushing the sand from the seat of her faded jeans.

"I see," Paul murmured. Then he frowned. "No, I don't see."

The woman laughed, and her face softened into real beauty. "No, I don't suppose you do. My name's Karen Mitchell," she said, extending her hand. "I own a bed-and-breakfast, and since the end of summer there haven't been many tourists in search of either."

Paul clasped her hand. "Paul Vanzant. And, coincidentally, I was on my way to your place."

The woman slanted a questioning look at him. "On the beach?" she asked in a skeptical tone.

"No. Of course not." Paul's lips twitched into a smile. "I was driving along, watching for your sign, and couldn't resist the lure of this stretch of shoreline." He lifted his shoulders again in that self-deprecating shrug. "I parked the car and started walking." He shifted his gaze toward the road and frowned. "My car's along there somewhere."

"Not in much of a hurry, are you?" Karen grinned.

"I gave up rushing for Lent."

"This is October." Her grin widened.

"I enjoyed it so much I extended it." Paul grinned back at her. "So, will you rent me a room?"

"But how did you know about my place?" Karen asked, playing for time while trying to decide if she should trust herself alone in the house with him.

Paul smiled in understanding and approval of her caution. "The taciturn proprietor of that picturesque general store in town recommended your place to me." He frowned, remembering. "Come to think of it, he said he'd give you a call and tell you to expect me."

His dry description of Calvin Muthard, owner of the one and only general store in the small nearby town, was so accurate that Karen didn't doubt for an instant that Paul had spoken to him. "When was that?"

Paul shrugged. "Thirty minutes or so."

"That explains it, then." Karen matched his shrug. "I've been out here on the beach for some time. If Calvin said he would call, then he called."

"You could give him a call," Paul suggested.

Karen's smile was wry. "Knowing Calvin, he'll keep ringing until he reaches me."

"So, will you rent me a room?"

"Why not?" Karen laughed. "I've got plenty of them, all empty."

"Good." Paul turned away. "I'll get my car and..." His voice trailed away and he turned to her, a smile on his lips. "Where *is* the house?"

Karen's ordinary brown eyes grew bright with amusement and were suddenly not at all ordinary. Tiny gold flecks sparked light in their dark depths, mesmerizing Paul for an electric instant. The odd moment was broken when she pointed to a building beyond the rocks and dunes.

"It's that monstrosity right there." She smiled at him over her shoulder. "You can't miss it, even if you want to."

The house was large and solid-looking. Victorian in design, it appeared to have weathered every storm nature had flung at it. Its dignified form appealed to Paul

"It's beautiful," he murmured, studying the structure. "I can't imagine how I missed it."

"I can." Karen's soft laugh caused an unusual tingling reaction at Paul's nape. "You were walking with your head down. The few times you did glance up, you stared out to sea."

"You were watching me?" Pondering the strange sensation at the back of his neck, Paul made a show of examining the veranda encircling the house.

"I'd tired of watching the gulls and talking to myself." Karen's voice retained a hint of laughter. "You were a diversion."

"You live in that house alone?" One eyebrow peaked as he shifted his gaze to her face.

Karen nodded. "For now."

Intrigued but unwilling to pry, Paul suppressed the questions that sprang to his tongue. "I'll get the car and meet you at the house." Pivoting, he headed for the road.

"I'll start a pot of coffee," she called after him.

"Great, I could use a cup," Paul shouted back, suddenly aware of the sharpness of the wind and the inadequacy of his poplin jacket.

The car was farther along the road than he had thought, and by the time he slid behind the wheel his fingers were numb with cold. Blowing warm breath into his cupped hands, Paul stared at the stretch of deserted road and frowned. Accustomed as he was to the noise and pace of city life, Paul could appreciate the solitude afforded by this empty section of the Maine coast. He himself had recently vacated a similar section. And yet for a woman to be on her own and living in a house that size . . . Paul's frown deepened. Was she safe here? A prickling of alarm startled him out of his introspection. It was none of his business, he thought impatiently, shoving the key into the ignition. How and where Karen Mitchell chose to live was no concern of his. Besides, he mused, driving the car off the soft shoulder and onto the road, she was no longer alone. He was here now.

The house was even more fascinating on closer inspection. Though definitely weathered-looking, it had none of the brooding quality one might expect of a large, isolated house surrounded by sand dunes and facing an ocean. Pulling the car onto the sandy drive at the side of the house, Paul killed the engine, then sat gazing at the building while attempting to identify its attraction.

Welcome. Haven. Security. Paul went still as the words rushed into his mind. He had been wandering aimlessly for months. Winter would soon eclipse fall. Was he subconsciously seeking a secure, welcoming haven? Had he also secretly hoped to find the warmth of a woman as well as the warmth of a solid shelter?

Ridiculous! Paul's aristocratic features set into forbidding lines. He owned two perfectly adequate homes, both equal in size to Karen's. And when he was ready he would go back, at least to his primary house in Philadelphia. As for hoping to find the warmth of a woman? Paul winced. He had not experienced even the slightest urge for a woman's company in a very long time. He had existed without that particular physical urge by necessity. He needed lodging, nothing more.

Yet there was a lure to this particular section of the coast, an attraction Paul had not felt during the weeks he'd spent in his son's cottage farther up the coast. That inexplicable lure was the reason he had pulled the car off the road to walk the deserted beach.

But the beach hadn't been deserted, Paul mused, narrowing his eyes as he stared at the large house. Was it Karen's magnetism that had been tugging at him? Paul blinked in surprise at the fanciful thought.

What utter nonsense! Paul shook his head to clear his mind. He was long past the age of believing in fateful attraction, if in fact he had ever been of an age to believe in it. The only lure here was the call of nature and a house reminiscent of another, gentler age, and it was a summons Paul didn't have the time to indulge. He had drifted, rudderless, for too long. It was time to get back to working—and living.

Staring at Karen Mitchell's house without really seeing it, Paul's thoughts wandered back to a time when he had enjoyed life, years before the death of his wife, an event that had occurred six months previously. Learning of his wife's infidelities had robbed his personal and business life of all the joy he'd derived from it. And yet Paul had continued, living a lie at home and at the office until the day his wife had driven her classic Corvette into a bridge abutment. At that point, he had literally dropped out. Within weeks he had formally retired from the banking work he loved and had closed the house in which he had laughed and loved and raised his two children. He had been wandering ever since.

Grimacing, Paul deliberately drew his gaze from the house. Peter was expecting to hear from him; and what his son was expecting to hear was that Paul was coming home, this time for good. He'd stay the night, then be on his way.

His dark eyes coolly remote, Paul swung the car door open and slid his tall body from the expensive vehicle. Striding purposefully to the back of the car, he removed only one of his cases from the trunk.

Karen swung the heavy door open as Paul mounted the veranda steps on the seaward side of the house. As he crossed the threshold the aroma of rich coffee, combined with the scent of an exciting female, assailed his senses. Against his will, Paul found himself inhaling both seductive fragrances.

"Are you hungry?" Karen asked as she closed the door, shutting out the rising wind.

"Yes." Paul smiled at the realization that he'd been unaware of his empty stomach until that minute. "As a matter of fact, I'm famished." His smile turned wry. "I believe I forgot to eat lunch."

"Well, then, just drop your bag here in the hall," she said briskly, indicating the spacious hallway connecting the identical doors. "Dinner won't be ready for several hours," she continued, turning away from the wide central staircase and walking toward an open doorway to her left. "But I can warm up some croissants for you to have with your coffee, if you'd like?" She paused in the doorway, eyebrows raised.

"I'd like that very much, thank you," Paul answered with stiff formality. He noted her speculative frown as he bent to set his suitcase at the foot of the stairs. Chiding himself for his coldness, he attempted a lighter tone. "Is there somewhere I can wash up?"

Karen's expression eased as she nodded. "There's the powder room." She motioned to a door to the right behind the staircase. A smile teased her lips. "Be careful, though. You're rather large and the room's rather small. You could bump into yourself by merely turning around."

Paul found the room every bit as small as she had warned it would be. A hint of a smile touched his lips as he washed his hands at the tiny sink. The powder room was an afterthought, he guessed, and had more than likely been a closet originally. The room wasn't much larger than a rest room on a commercial jet plane. Paul imagined Karen in the cramped space, and his smile broadened to reveal strong white teeth.

Sharing the room with her would be interesting, he reflected, if not downright adventurous.

A shocking stab of sensual awareness sobered him. Staring at his reflection in the mirror above the sink, Paul was amazed at the color tingeing the taut skin over his high cheekbones. His appetite was suddenly sharp, but not for warm croissants. He wanted a woman. Paul frowned at his dark-eyed image. No, he wanted a particular woman! The sensual awareness tightened inside him, tensing every sinew and muscle in his body.

Incredible. Paul closed his eyes and savored the painfully pleasant sensation of arousal coursing through him. He had been convinced his wife had dealt a death blow to his natural sex drive long before her own demise. And now to discover his mind and body reactivated and humming with anticipation because of an errant thought about a full-figured woman in a minuscule powder room was more than incredible, it was astonishing and damned funny!

So why aren't you laughing? Paul silently demanded of his somber reflection. It couldn't be that after all this time you've forgotten how to approach a woman with the intention of seduction, could it? Drawing a deep breath, Paul stared into the mirror and watched his features lock and his lips twist derisively. No, he hadn't forgotten, but seduction was for young, eager men, and he was no longer either.

Paul shrugged his shoulders and turned away from the mirror, bumping his lean hip on the edge of the sink as he moved. Laughing softly, he eased his tall frame from the room. The exciting inner tension was gone; Paul couldn't help but wonder if it would return.

It slammed into his midsection like a body blow the instant he stepped into the kitchen to find Karen bending to remove a tray from the oven. The faded jeans hugged her firm, rounded bottom. His breathing suddenly shallow, Paul fought an urge to cross the room and stroke his palms over that enticing curve. Fortunately, Karen decided the inner battle by straightening before he could make a move.

"Take off your jacket and sit down," she said, sliding a small tray of steaming croissants onto the stovetop. "And help yourself to the coffee," she added, inclining her head toward the glass coffeepot and cups on the table.

Aroused again and relieved at the opportunity to sit down, Paul still managed to remember his manners. "Can I help you there?" he asked, inching toward the table.

"No, thank you." Karen shot a quick smile over her shoulder as she transferred the hot pastries from the tray to a napkin-lined basket. "But you can pour a cup of coffee for me, please."

"Of course." Shrugging out of the jacket, Paul draped it over the back of a chair as he slid onto the seat. To his amazement, he found his hands steady as he poured coffee into the two cups. Applying mind over matter, he had his responsive body under control by the time she sat down opposite him.

"Smells delicious," he murmured, inhaling the aroma of the hot croissants.

"Help yourself," she invited. "There's butter and preserves." She indicated the containers with a flick of her hand as she reached for her cup.

"Not joining me?" Paul asked, breaking one of the crescent-shaped rolls.

"No." Karen shook her head. "I'm on a perpetual diet, and midafternoon croissants are not a part of it." Lifting her cup, she sipped at the steaming black coffee.

"Diet?" Paul paused in the act of slathering wild-strawberry preserves onto a piece of the roll. His frowning gaze made a brief survey of the upper half of her body; his memory retained a clear vision of the lower half. "You don't need to diet." The sincerity of his tone was proof that he was not merely being gallant.

"Oh, but I do." Karen's smile held an odd, bitter slant. "I love to cook and I love to eat," she said in a flat voice. "I pay for my indulgence in pounds... usually around my hips."

Personally, Paul considered her rounded hips uncomfortably alluring. Prudently he kept his thoughts to himself. "My problem's the direct opposite," he said for the sake of conversation. "I often forget to eat, and I have to remind myself to do so to keep from losing weight." He popped the bite of roll into his mouth and chewed with relish.

Her expression mocking, Karen cradled her cup in her palms and leaned back in her chair. "I should have such a problem," she drawled, tilting her cup in a silent salute. Her gaze boldly noted the breadth of his shoulders and chest and the evidence of well-developed muscles beneath his bulky knit sweater.

"For all the lack of nourishment, you appear to be in great shape."

Paul's smile was wry. "For my age, you mean?"

"For any age," she retorted. "How old are you?" There was a hint of challenge in her voice.

"I'll never see fifty again." Paul smiled at her look of genuine astonishment and tossed her challenge back at her. "How old are you?"

"I'll never see thirty again," she said in a dry tone. "As a matter of fact, I celebrated my thirty-seventh birthday last Tuesday."

Something, some infinitesimal inflection in her voice, alerted Paul. "Alone?" he guessed.

Karen hesitated, then sighed. "Yes."

"You have no family?" Paul probed gently, not sure exactly why he was bothering.

"I have two sons," she said brightly—too brightly. "They're away at school. I . . . received lovely birthday cards from them." Her smile was as bright as her tone, and as suspect. "Do you have children?" she asked swiftly, allowing him no time to question her further.

"Yes, two also," Paul answered. "I have a son and a daughter, both grown and married." Memory softened his expression.

"Grandchildren?" Karen guessed.

Paul's smile was gentle. "Yes, a six-week-old grandson from my son and daughter-in-law, and my daughter is currently a lady-in-waiting. The child is due at Christmas, on or about their first wedding anniversary."

"That's nice," she murmured, blinking as she glanced away. "I love babies."

Once again, Paul became alert to an odd tone in her voice. For a moment she looked so lost, so unhappy, that he had to squash the urge to go to her and draw her into his arms. "Your husband?" he asked very softly.

"I'm divorced." She turned to look at him as she stood up. The vulnerability was gone; an invisible curtain had been drawn, concealing her feelings. "If you've finished, I'll show you to your room." Her voice was steady, free of inflection.

Paul had the strange sensation of having been shoved outside, into the deepening dusk and frigid wind. The sensation disturbed him more than a little. Why it should bother him was baffling. He had grown used to being in the cold and the dark with the opposite sex. His wife Carolyn had kept him there for years. Feeling a chill, Paul tossed down the last of his coffee and stood up. "Ready when you are," he said in an even tone, plucking his jacket from the back of the chair.

Following Karen up the wide staircase proved to be a test of endurance for Paul. She had a lovely, graceful stride, shoulders back without being stiff, spine straight without being rigid, and her hips had a gentle, unpracticed sway that profoundly affected every one of his senses. Sweetly erotic images flashed through his mind as he trailed her down the hall, his darkened gaze fixed on the movement of her hips. His mind smoky from the heat of his thoughts, Paul was only vaguely aware of the room she ushered him into. The inflectionless sound of her voice pierced the sensuous fog.

"Of course, if this room doesn't suit you, you may choose any of the other six guest rooms," she was saying, moving to the long windows to pull the drapes open. "I thought this would be best since it has its own bathroom and looks out over the beach and the ocean." She swept her arm toward the view as if offering him a gift.

"This will be fine." Paul glanced around the room without really seeing it as he dutifully walked to stand beside her at the window. Darkness cloaked the land, and low-hanging clouds obscured the moon and stars. Paul could see very little except for outlines and the curling white of cresting waves. But standing this close to her he could smell her distinct scent, and his body tightened in response to it. Relief shivered through him when she moved away.

"Well, then," Karen said briskly. "I'll get bed linens and towels. It'll only take a minute to make up the bed." She was walking from the room before she'd finished speaking.

Keeping his back squarely to the room, Paul stared into the night, his thoughts just as black. What was wrong with him? he wondered bleakly, clenching his fists as he heard her reenter the room. He was reacting to Karen like a teenager with a hormonal explosion. He wanted to grab her, touch her—everywhere. He wanted to kiss her, bite her, thrust his tongue into her sweet mouth! Oh, God, how he wanted! Paul was shuddering inside when the snapping sound of a sheet being shaken dispelled the erotic thoughts teasing his senses.

"Is there something I can help you with?" Paul closed his eyes, despairing of the hoarse sound in his voice.

"No, thank you, I'm just about finished." Karen's tone had an edge that tugged at his attention, an edge that held a hint of—what? Trepidation? Outright fear?

Raising his eyelids fractionally, Paul turned slowly to face her. Moving swiftly, economically, her hands smoothed a candlewick bedspread over two plump pillows. On closer inspection, he thought he detected a slight tremor in her competent hands. Was Karen afraid of him? Paul mused, watching as she carried a stack of towels into the adjoining bathroom. Had she sensed his reaction to her, and was she now regretting renting him the room?

Avoiding his eyes, Karen walked into the room and directly to the door to the hallway, by her manner convincing Paul his speculations were correct.

"I'll leave you to get settled in," she said, reminding him of a wary doe as she hesitated in the doorway. "Dinner will be ready at 7:30." Turning abruptly, she strode from the room.

"Thank you." A grimace twisted Paul's mouth as he realized he was speaking to thin air; Karen had fled. A sick despair sank heavily to the pit of his stomach. She was afraid of him, he thought, raking a hand through his hair in frustration. Dammit! The last thing he'd wanted was to frighten her. Sighing, Paul turned to stare into the unwelcoming darkness of a cold night.

Karen was also staring into the night. Directly across the hall, in a room that was a twin to his, she stood at the window, her trembling fingers clutching the old-fashioned carved wood frame. Her breathing was ragged and uneven; her stomach felt queasy.

What had come over her? The silent cry battered her mind. Her senses were jangling; her emotions were freaking out! And all because of a man who was almost twenty years her senior!

But, oh, glory, what a man! Shutting her eyes tightly, Karen shivered deliciously in response to the image of him that consumed her mind. Aristocratic. Patrician. Handsome. Cultured. Endearingly preoccupied. The adjectives crashed into each other as they rushed forward. At fifty-whatever, Paul Vanzant was the most compelling man Karen had ever met.

And he probably thinks you're an absolute idiot! A sigh whispered through her lips as Karen accepted the mental rebuke. She was thirty-seven years old and the mother of two teenage sons. She had experienced the satisfaction of a successful career and—though briefly—the love of a dynamic man on the way up. She was well educated and well traveled. And she had conducted herself with all the aplomb of a wide-eyed, tongue-tied, backward young girl being presented at court.

But Lord, the man was *fantastic*! Feeling as if she were melting inside, Karen tightened her grip on the windowframe and leaned forward to press her forehead against the cold pane. She longed to stroke the white wings highlighting his black hair at his temples— No! She longed to stroke the entire length of his tall, muscular body. Sensual awareness flared to life, and she quivered in response to the mere thought of touching Paul.

Was she losing her mind? Or had she simply been too long alone? It had been five years since Karen had been with a man, five years since the separation and subsequent divorce that had shredded the fabric of her marriage and life. Embittered, she had embraced celibacy, not grown frustrated because of it. Karen hadn't wanted anything to do with a man, and she certainly hadn't wanted to share intimacy with one.

Intimacy. Karen moaned softly as the word echoed inside her whirling mind. Male-female intimacy meant silken touches and deep, hungry kisses and an even deeper, all-consuming possession.

Suddenly weak and shaking, Karen turned her head to press her flushed cheek to the cool window. With her mind's eye she could see Paul, naked and beautiful, his dark eyes shadowed by passion, a sensuous smile on his sculpted masculine lips.

"Yes, yes."

The jagged, breathless sound of her own voice startled Karen into awareness. Breathing deeply, she glanced around in confusion. What in the world was she doing? Her face grew hot and then cold at the answer. Her movements jerky and uncoordinated, she walked to the low double dresser and picked up her hairbrush. Drawing the brush through her wind-tossed curls, she frowned at the slumbrous glow in the brown eyes reflected in the mirror. Was this the same self-contained woman who had turned her back on her career and all her activities in the city to return to her childhood home? Karen wondered tiredly. Could the woman in the mirror possibly be the same person who had determinedly removed herself physically and mentally from the pleasures of the flesh?

Karen shook her head and dropped the brush onto the dresser. This would not do. Paul was, for whatever reason, obviously in transit. He would stay a while, and then he would go. And unless she was very careful, he could take a part of her with him. Karen knew she could not let that happen.

She was vulnerable to him. Why she was vulnerable to this particular man was unimportant—at least for the moment. She had to get herself firmly under control. Paul Vanzant was the stuff dreams were made of, she decided sadly. And dreams of that sort were for the young and innocent, not the wise and embittered.

Drawing a deep breath, Karen squared her shoulders and smiled at her reflected image. "He's in his fifties," she said in a soft but bracing tone. "He has grown children, and he's a grandfather. Children and grandchildren presuppose a mother and grandmother. Where is she?" A spasm of pain flicked across Karen's face. "He's on the move, you fool!" she chided her image. "His wife is more than likely at home, playing the doting grandma." She shut her eyes against the sting of tears and closed her mind to the bittersweet yearning to fill the emptiness of her body and arms with a tiny new life. Denying the image of a child with Paul's aristocratic features in miniature, she opened her eyes again, wide. "He's too old for a serious new commitment. He's too old to be running around while his wife sits waiting at home. And he's too old for you."

Feeling like the idiot she'd accused herself of being, Karen spun away from the dresser, unwilling to face the sad-eyed woman reflected in the mirror above it. She had work to do. There was laundry in the dryer to be folded, and a wet load waiting to be transferred to it from the washer. She had to scrub potatoes for baking and clean and chop vegetables for a salad. She had to make a batch of biscuits. She didn't have time to indulge in fantasies about a man she had met less than two hours before and knew absolutely nothing about. She had to get her house and head together.

Acting on the thought, Karen rushed from her bedroom and down the wide staircase. She flicked on the radio in the kitchen on her way through to the laundry room. Throughout the following hours, coherent thought was held at bay by the blaring racket and agonizing screams commonly referred to as "heavy metal."

Karen had a blasting headache, but her chores—and the potatoes—were done. She had showered and dressed in a silky overblouse and a flattering, if practical, denim skirt. Her hair was brushed into soft gleaming waves; a minimum of makeup enhanced her clear, naturally pale face. The table was set in the small dining alcove and the scallops were simmering in an aromatic sauterne butter sauce under the broiler. The noise issuing from the radio ceased abruptly. Spinning around, Karen glared at the tall, too-attractive cause of her feverish activity.

"Why did you do that?" she demanded aggressively, quickly gliding a glance over the appeal of his body, which was clad in casual but obviously expensive pants and a white sweater.

"Why?" Paul repeated in disbelief. "To prevent both deafness and madness," he answered in a scathing tone. "I was beginning to think I'd walked into bedlam."

"The music keeps me company," she retorted.

"It'll turn your brain to mush," he snapped. "I thought you were an intelligent, sensible woman. You can't possibly enjoy that . . . that . . ."

"Noise?" Karen supplied the applicable word, sighing inwardly at her erratic behavior. "No, actually I hate it."

"But then why play it?" Paul slowly crossed the room to her.

Karen held her ground but withdrew inwardly. "Because I was dissatisfied with my own thoughts," she admitted. "And the noise blanked them out."

Compassion softened his tight features. "You were thinking about your children?" he asked softly.

Feeling not an ounce of shame, Karen clutched at the excuse. "Yes, I was missing my children." There was a grain of truth to her assertion, she assured herself, meeting his compassionate gaze boldly. For had her boys been in the house that afternoon, she probably wouldn't have been sitting on the beach and so would not have met him and thus would not have found herself wildly attracted to him in the first place. The rationale was unpalatable to Karen, but it was the best she could come up with on the spur of the moment.

Chapter Two

Y ou do a mean scallop scampi.''

"Thank you." Karen glanced up at Paul, an uncertain smile hovering at the corners of her lips. The compliment, coming so unexpectedly after his near-total silence during the meal, both pleased and confused her. "I'm glad you enjoyed it."

"I did," he said, pausing a moment before continuing, "I enjoyed it very much, even though I realize I wasn't very good company throughout the consumption of it."

Karen lifted her shoulders in a half shrug. "Conversation is not a guest requirement."

Paul smiled. "Perhaps it should be."

"Perhaps." Karen frowned and shrugged again. "But if a guest is preoccupied..."

"This particular guest is preoccupied by speculation about his hostess."

"Me!" she exclaimed, experiencing an odd thrill of excitement.

"Yes, you." Refilling his coffee cup from the carafe she'd placed on the table, Paul leaned back in his chair and gazed at her intently.

"But what about me?" Karen shook her head impatiently. "I mean, what were you speculating about?"

"The fact that you're living alone in this large house, for one thing," Paul answered, indicating the entire building with a flick of his hand.

Karen followed his hand motion with her eyes. "I was born in this house," she murmured.

"Which explains absolutely nothing."

"I wasn't aware of owing—" she began, her voice strained.

Paul interrupted her. "Of course you don't owe me a thing, especially explanations, but that doesn't preclude my curiosity about you." He shrugged and smiled; the smile got to her.

"Okay, I'll indulge your curiosity." Karen inclined her head in thanks as he filled her coffee cup. Cradling the warmed china in her palms, she sat back and smiled. "Fire away."

Paul's lips curved with wry amusement and a hint of suggestiveness. "On any subject?"

"I won't guarantee an answer," Karen drawled, "but you can give it your best shot."

His laughter was slow in starting but rapidly grew into an attractive rumble that filled the small dining alcove, and Karen, with warmth. The room absorbed the sound, and so did Karen. A delicious tremor shivered through her as he raised his cup in a salute.

"Now I'm intimidated." Paul sounded anything but intimidated. He chuckled at the look she gave him. "I don't know if this is my best shot, but to begin, why are you all alone in this large leftover from another era?"

That one was easy, and Karen responded immediately. "Actually, I've only been alone for a few weeks. I employ three people, two women and one man, during the season." She smiled dryly. "In fact, the house is, or was, in effect closed until spring."

"But the proprietor of that store said—"

Karen cut in to ask gently, "Exactly what did Calvin say?"

Paul frowned in concentration. "He said, well, just maybe you'd be willing to rent me a room for a night or two." Paul mimicked Calvin's Yankee twang.

Karen laughed in appreciation of his effort. "Precisely. Calvin knows full well that I close the place at the end of September, and he admitted as much."

"You spoke to him?"

Karen nodded. "While I was finishing dinner. I did tell you he'd persist until he reached me."

"Yes, you did," Paul confirmed, beginning to frown. "So, what's your verdict?" His dark eyebrows peaked. "Are you planning to toss me out on my, er . . . ear the minute I step away from this table, or have you decided to let me stay the night?"

"You may stay—" she paused to grin "—as long as you like. It appears that you made quite a good impression on Calvin."

"Indeed?" Paul managed not to laugh.

"Oh, yes, indeed." Karen didn't manage it; she laughed softly. "And, as Calvin is generally an excellent judge of character, I'll accept his recommendation."

"I knew there was something I liked about that dour-faced, hard-nosed Yankee," Paul commented drolly.

Swallowing her laughter at his deadly accurate description of Calvin, Karen pushed back her chair and stood up. "Question period over?" she murmured hopefully, beginning to gather the dishes together.

"Over!" Paul exclaimed, rising quickly to help clear the table. "I've only asked one question."

"Well, then," she sighed loudly, "can we put it on hold until after cleaning up? I detest clutter." She frowned at the littered table.

"Certainly." Paul nodded. "I'll even assist." His gaze trailed hers to the table, and his mouth curved into a grimace. "I can't abide clutter, either."

Oddly, knowing they shared one small trait made Karen feel closer to Paul. And, though she told herself she was being silly, the feeling eased the reluctance she was experiencing about being questioned further by him.

Two pairs of competent hands dealt swiftly with the dinner debris, freeing them of the chore within minutes. With the dishwasher swishing in the background, Paul opened the bottle of white wine Karen produced, while she retrieved two stemmed glasses from the lovingly cared-for hundred-year-old hutch in the formal dining room. Carrying the bottle casually by its long neck, Paul strolled into the spacious living room; Karen followed after giving the kitchen one last critical appraisal.

Ensconced in a wide-armed, deeply cushioned easy chair, Paul offered Karen a wry smile as she settled into the corner of the matching sofa. As he poured out the wine, he put her own thoughts into words.

"It would appear that we have at least one thing in common," he said. "We are both apparently overly tidy people."

Karen's smile matched his in wryness. "Why do I get the sneaky feeling that you've also been accused of being a fussbudget?"

The bottle went still, poised over the glass. The stream of clear liquid ceased flowing. Paul slowly raised his gaze to meet hers. The light of impish humor glowed in the dark depths of his eyes.

"You, too, huh?" When Karen nodded, he grinned. "My daughter Nicole once told me that though I wasn't exactly clean-crazy, I most definitely was straighten-up-nuts."

Karen's laugh of delight rippled through the room, adding a dimension of comfort unrelated to the bright down-home decor. "I think I'd like your Nicole," she said when the amusement subsided. "She sounds like fun."

"She is now, because she's happy." Paul's expression was somber. "But there was a period, a very long period, when she seemed barely alive, never mind fun."

There was no way Karen could let his statement pass. Reaching to accept the glass he held out to her, she voiced her interest. "There was a time when your daughter was unhappy?" For some inexplicable reason, she couldn't imagine a child of Paul's being unhappy—which was really silly, Karen knew. Most children suffered periods of unhappiness for one reason or another.

Paul's hesitation was brief but telling. He obviously didn't want to discuss his daughter. "Nicole was involved in an auto accident some years ago," he said finally. "She withdrew from life, from her family, while she worked out the aftereffects of the damage." The minute emphasis he placed on the words *her family* spoke volumes about his own worry and anxiety during that period.

"She was handicapped?" Karen asked softly, even as she told herself to let it go.

"She was a model," Paul said slowly. "A rather famous model. The crash left her face, neck and shoulder scarred." His tone, or rather the complete lack of it, revealed much about the anguish he'd felt at the time.

Still, Karen couldn't let the subject drop; she had to ask. "But she's all right now?"

Paul's lips curved into a gentle, contented smile. "Yes, she's more than all right. Nicole's not only happy, she is deeply in love with her husband." Parental love and pride glowed from his softened dark eyes.

"I'm glad," Karen said, simply but with utter sincerity. "And your son?" She was completely aware that the roles of questioner and questionee had been neatly reversed; she hoped to keep it that way. A small smile teased her lips as the glow brightened in his eyes. It was obvious to Karen that Paul unconditionally adored his son. Being in the same emotional condition concerning her own boys, she could appreciate the pride shining from his eyes.

"My son Peter is—special." Paul went still as his eyes widened fractionally. "Good Lord!" he muttered.

"What?" Even though his voice had been low, the tone of it affected Karen like a shout. "What is it?" she asked, glancing around as if she expected to see a visible cause for his distress.

Paul gave a sharp shake of his head. "I told Peter I'd call him this evening." He sighed. "And now I've very likely got both Peter and his wife Patricia worried."

Not quite understanding his agitation, Karen motioned toward the hallway. "There's a phone less than ten feet away from you in the hall. Be my guest."

Paul's expression changed instantly. A teasing gleam sprang into his eyes to banish the shadow of concern. "It's a long-distance call. My son lives in Philadelphia."

Karen sipped her wine daintily before responding in a dry tone. "I'm in an expansive mood." She indicated the foyer with a negligent wave. "Better take advantage of it. It doesn't happen often."

"You're a bit austere with the purse strings?"

"Nooo..." Karen drew the word out slowly. "I'm a true product of my New England upbringing and *very* austere with the purse strings." Her soft lips tightened. "It was one of the biggest bones of contention between me and Charles."

"Charles?" That one softly spoken word from Paul reversed the roles again.

Karen sighed into her delicate glass and took a deep, fortifying swallow. "Charles Mitchell."

"Your former husband?"

She nodded once, then attempted to deflect the question she could see hovering on his lips. "Aren't you going to make that call?"

Paul's slow smile sent Karen's hopes crashing down in flames. "It'll keep until morning. So will Peter. I'll catch him at the office."

She gave it one last shot. "But you said they'll worry."

"They're used to it." His drawl was heavy. "They've been angsting over me for nearly six months. Another night won't make much difference either way."

His enigmatic statement sank a solid hook into Karen's already aroused interest in him. She wanted to know everything, anything, about him. Paul didn't allow her the seconds needed to sort her queries into a semblance of order.

"You were telling me about Charles," he said, scattering her thoughts.

"I was?" She gulped at her wine and suddenly the glass was empty. Frowning at it, she held it out for re-filling.

"Well, no," Paul admitted, tipping the bottle over her glass. "But I was hoping you would." Topping off his own glass, he lounged in the roomy chair and offered her a bland, innocent look.

Karen wasn't fooled for an instant; but she did feel inordinately thirsty. After several more deep swallows of the wine, her tongue loosened considerably. "What exactly did you hope to find out?" She didn't hear the fuzzy sound of her voice, but Paul did. He fought the urge to smile.

"Would it be terribly crass of me to admit to hoping to hear the entire story?"

"Terribly," Karen muttered into her glass before taking another gulp. "But as I said, I'm in a strange, expansive mood tonight."

Not to mention slightly into your cups. Paul decided Karen was both cute and attractive with her Yankee edges blurred, but prudently kept his thoughts to himself. "Then I'll be crass and ask for the story, from the beginning."

Karen worked at an affronted expression and failed miserably. To salve her feelings, she took another sip of wine. "I met Charles Mitchell while in my junior year of college in Boston." Her lips twisted self-mockingly. "I was in love, married and two months pregnant before the start of my senior year. Needless to say, I never did graduate."

Pondering the twinge of emotion he felt stab at his midsection, Paul kept his tone free of inflection. "Go on."

"Life was wonderful for ten years—love, marriage, the two sons resulting from it and even the career I embarked on when Rand, my oldest, and Mark, my baby, were seven and five respectively." Her sigh was revealing and hurt Paul in a way he didn't understand. "At least I believed it was wonderful."

"Charles didn't?" he probed softly.

Karen shook her head. She certainly was excessively dry. She allowed herself another sip of the wine. "You must understand, Charles worked very hard. He was always dynamic, ambitious. It was part of his charm. Everyone knew he was going places.'' She suddenly needed another, deeper swallow of wine. ''The problem was, Charles was going places with several different women.''

''What? You tolerated that?''

Karen's body jerked in reaction to the sharpness of Paul's voice.

''Tolerated?'' Karen stared at him blankly, beginning to really feel the effects of her unaccustomed self-indulgence. Then his question registered. ''I didn't know!'' she cried in self-defense. ''I was so . . . so stupidly happy, I never dreamed . . .'' Her voice gave way to tense silence as she noticed the uncanny stillness gripping Paul. What had she said to induce that stark expression on his handsome face? She closed her eyes and shook her head. When she opened her eyes, his expression was bland, free of strain. Had she imagined his look of near agony? Paul didn't allow her the time to work it out in her cloudy mind.

''Don't tell me, let me guess,'' he drawled sarcastically. ''A close friend dropped the hint that set you thinking and doubting and finally confirming. Right?''

There was something in his tone, a tip-off to what he was thinking, but . . . Karen shook her head. Her senses were too fogged to permit in-depth thought. Instead, she sighed and answered his query. ''No. If they knew, and I feel certain they did, my friends were too full of concern about hurting me.'' Her smile was tired. ''Charles told me.''

''The bastard.'' Though Paul's voice was little more than a murmured snarl, Karen heard it.

"Yeah." The twang was thick and uncontrived. Her shoulders lifted, then dropped. The action said reams more than mere words would have. She tipped the glass to her trembling lips while a voice within her silently asked how in the hell she'd gotten into this discussion and, more importantly, why?

"Karen?" The edge of concern in his voice was obvious. "Are you all right?"

"Dandy," Karen quipped, swallowing an unladylike hiccup. "I think I may be slightly smashed, but I'm just dandy."

Paul's smile was gentle with compassion. "You don't drink much as a rule, do you?"

"Much?" Karen giggled. "I rarely drink at all. I keep the wine in stock for the paying guests." She gazed at him with cloudy-eyed intent. "It has a tendency to unhinge the mind and loosen the tongue, doesn't it?"

"Hmm," Paul murmured. "But not to worry, you're safe."

Deeper and deeper. Karen narrowed her eyes. What was he telling her—without telling her? Was she safe because he simply wasn't interested? But that didn't equate, she told herself, remembering the strength of the vibrations his body had transmitted to hers almost from the moment they'd met. Or had the attraction all been from one side—hers? The thought was almost sobering...almost. And at the moment the thoughts were all just too much effort.

"I want to sleep." Her childlike request bounced off rock.

"No, you don't." There wasn't an ounce of give in Paul's voice.

"Yes, I do." Karen sniffed and blinked owlishly. "I'm so sleepy." Moving very carefully, she set her glass aside and stumbled to her feet. "If you'll excuse me, I think I'll go on up." She started toward the hall, the mere fact of her forgotten glass saying more than words about her condition.

"Stay right where you are." The tone of authority in Paul's voice halted her abruptly at the base of the wide stairway. Not even in her tipsy state could Karen consider disobeying his arresting command.

"Paul, please." Turning her head slowly, carefully, for the room had suddenly begun to sway, Karen gave him a weary look. "I must lie down."

Paul rose as he set his own glass aside. "No, Karen." He shook his head gently as he walked to her. "Chances are that if you sleep now you'll wake up sick. What you need is some exercise in the fresh air."

"Exercise!" Karen moaned. "Fresh air! You mean—like outside?"

"Yes." Paul was not altogether successful in masking his amusement.

"But it's cold outside!"

"You forgot 'baby.'"

"What?" Karen glowered at him.

"Forget it." His lips twitched. "You'll need a coat, a warm one. Where would it be?"

Still glowering, Karen motioned distractedly at the closet inside the front door. "There's a navy peacoat in there somewhere."

Eyeing her narrowly, Paul reached for the closet door. "If you bolt for the stairs, I'll catch you," he warned, reading her intentions correctly. When her shoulders slumped in defeat, he turned to rummage inside the closet. He found the jacket on a hook near the back of the closet and a navy-blue knit cap on a shelf above the row of hooks.

Tired, fuzzy and thoroughly cowed, Karen stood docilely while Paul buttoned her into the jacket and tugged the hat onto her head and over her ears. When he turned to steer her along the hall to the side door that led to the beach, she tilted her head to run a misty-eyed glance over his sweater. It was warm, but not warm enough.

"What about you?" she muttered, stepping by him onto the veranda and immediately gasping at the chill wind that stole her breath. "Where's your coat?"

"Close at hand." Grasping her upper arm, Paul descended the veranda steps and walked to the side of his car parked in the sandy driveway. Pulling the back door open, he withdrew a down-filled nylon ski jacket. "I tossed this onto the back seat when it warmed up today about noon."

"I see." She didn't, of course. Karen didn't see or understand anything. A frown tugging her delicate eyebrows together, she watched as he shrugged into the brown-and-white jacket. She began to move automatically when he started walking toward the beach. "Where were you coming from today?" she gasped, quick-stepping to keep up with his long stride. "And please slow down!"

Paul shortened his gait at once and slanted an apologetic smile at her. "I'm sorry. What was your question?" His innocent tone didn't fool her for a second. Karen was slightly tipsy—she wasn't unconscious.

"You heard."

His laughter was low, and too darned attractive. "I was coming from farther up the coast." He hesitated, as if in silent debate about continuing. Then he shrugged. "I'd spent the past couple of weeks in the small place my son owns up there. I closed it for the winter this morning."

Paul released his hold on her and draped his arm around her shoulders as they approached a high sand dune. Plowing through the loose sand, they moved as one around the dune and down onto the more solidly packed sand on the beach.

"And you're heading for Philadelphia?" she asked, breathing a little easier as they attained firmer ground.

"Yes." He paused, bringing her to a stop as he stared out at the white-tipped, inky sea. "It's time I went back to work."

"What kind of work do you do?" Following his lead, she turned when he did, feeling her low shoes sink into the moist sand as they strolled along, inches from the lapping wavelets.

"I was a banker."

Karen was not surprised; Paul looked like a banker. "Was?" she prompted, growing less fuzzy as the brisk breeze dispersed the aftereffects of the wine.

"We can talk about that later," Paul said, a trifle imperiously. "I want to hear about your ex-husband."

"Oh, Paul," she sighed.

"You started it, now finish." His tone was unrelenting. "What did you mean when you said he told you about the other women?"

"Exactly that." Karen's shoulders moved in an uncomfortable shrug. "After over ten years of marriage, Charles came to me requesting—no, demanding—a more modern, civilized relationship.'' Her voice betrayed her tightening throat. Even after five years, the memory had the power to infuriate her.

''Continue.''

Paul's terse tone pierced the haze of anger in Karen's mind. She exhaled sharply. ''I didn't, truly didn't, understand what he was talking about. Charles was happy to enlighten me.'' A shudder rippled through her body, and Karen felt grateful for the weight of Paul's arm around her shoulder, tightening to steady her. ''He said that a modern, civilized marriage should never include the restrictive bonds of fidelity.''

Paul was quiet, too quiet. Karen could feel the tension tautening his muscles, but before she could question him he again nudged her into speech.

''Finish. Get it out of your system.''

''There isn't much more. He suggested we stay together, as a family, but that we both—'' her voice went flat and hard ''—share the wealth, as it were.''

At any other time, the viciousness of Paul's curse might have shocked Karen, but on a dark beach, in a darker frame of mind, she endorsed the expletive.

''Since you're here, alone, I'm assuming you told him no.''

''I told him to go to hell.''

''Bravo.''

Paul's one word of approval and praise warmed Karen throughout the hour they trudged through the sand in companionable silence. She didn't know why his commendation warmed her; she only knew that it did.

"And your sons?" Paul broke the unstrained silence as they were shrugging out of their jackets. "How did they react?"

Karen blamed her shiver on the chilly wind and managed a faint smile. "Who ever knows with children? There are moments I tell myself that they are handling it all very well." She lost the smile. "And then there are other times I feel positive they are blaming me because I left their father." Feeling the sting of incipient tears, she swung away, heading for the kitchen. "How about a cup of hot chocolate?"

The subject was closed; Paul accepted her decision. "I'd prefer tea," he said easily, strolling into the room behind her. "Less calories, you know." His teasing ploy worked, drawing a genuine smile from her.

"Tea it is." Karen started for the stove, then paused to glance at him over her shoulder. "And, Paul, thanks for insisting on the walk. It helped."

"Feeling better? Less disoriented?"

"Yes." She actually laughed. "If a little foolish."

"Not necessary." He crossed the brick-tiled floor, coming to a stop mere inches away from her. "We're all allowed our weak moments."

Karen lowered her eyes. "But perhaps we should have them when we're alone."

"I'll never tell." He raised her chin with the tip of one finger. His smile was heartwarmingly tender. "How about that tea?"

Karen felt amazingly good the next morning. Humming to herself as she prepared breakfast, she reiterated her last thought before sleep had caught up to her the previous night; *Paul Vanzant was a very nice man . . . and darned sexy, too!*

Smiling, she turned away from the stove, intending to dash up the stairs and knock on his bedroom door to tell him that breakfast was almost ready. Paul strode through the back door before she could take the first step.

"Something smells good." He smiled and inhaled deeply. "No, everything smells good."

Karen laughed. "I thought you were still asleep. I was just going to rouse you."

"I've been up for hours," he said, shrugging out of his jacket as he went toward the hall closet. *And I've been aroused ever since I got here!* Paul kept the thought to himself, savoring the sensation like a warm fire on a bitter day. He was feeling good. Wrong! He was feeling great. His mood was infectious. He had Karen laughing easily moments after returning to the kitchen.

"How 'bout a walk?" he asked the minute they'd finished eating.

"I have work to do!" Karen protested, though not too strongly.

"Like what?"

She held up one hand, ticking off fingers as she listed the day's chores. "Dusting. Laundry. Bed-making."

Paul gave her a considering look, then nodded once. "Okay. I'll help. We'll cut the chores in half."

"But you're a guest!"

"Big deal." He grinned; she melted. "I'll help you clean these breakfast things away. Then I'll do the beds while you start the laundry. And then . . ." He grinned again at her bemused expression. "I'll call Peter while you do the dusting." He snapped his fingers. "Nothing to it."

"Are you always this organized?" Karen scuffed the toe of her running shoe in the sand, just to break the smooth surface, and slanted a questioning glance at the tall man pacing beside her. It was their second walk of that day. Long rays of afternoon sunlight bounced a glitter off the undulating sea that almost stung the eye. Working together, she and Paul had wiped out her chore list for the entire week, except for the trip to the supermarket in town.

"It's atavistic." Paul laughed down at her. "I come from a long line of fussily neat, well-organized Dutch folk."

"Oh, brother!" Karen rolled her eyes.

"Hey, don't complain." His laughter deepened. "The work's done, isn't it?"

"All except dinner, which won't get done unless I get back to the house pretty quick," she retorted with her innate New England practicality.

"I give up." Paul pivoted on his heel. "Let's go make dinner." He walked so fast that Karen could barely breathe, let alone protest his intent. But she dug in her heels the instant they walked into the house.

"I'll cook dinner," she declared, planting her hands on her hips. "You go take a shower or read the paper or, better yet, try your son once more."

Paul appeared about to argue until she made the last suggestion. Having made two failed attempts to contact his son, he was feeling a trifle concerned. "Right." He nodded. "I'll try Peter again." He swung away, but paused in the doorway. "It's been a good day, Karen. Hasn't it?"

Karen's smile was soft, as was her voice. "A very good day, Paul. Thank you for it."

"No thanks necessary. The day was free. Ours to take." He grew still, a frown drawing his dark brows together. Then he smiled. "As all the days are, by damn!" Striding back to her, he grasped her upper arms, drew her to him and kissed her gently on the mouth. When he raised his head, a smile curved his lips. "That was even better than the walk." Releasing her abruptly, he strode from the room.

Startled, delighted, Karen stared at the empty doorway, a bemused look on her kiss-softened face. Lifting her hand, she touched the tip of her fingers to her tingling lips.

"By damn!" she murmured in a tone of wonder.

Chapter Three

You are an excellent cook." Lifting his wineglass, Paul tilted it in a silent salute before drinking the last pale drops. "The broiled scrod was every bit as delicious as last night's scampi."

"Thank you." Pleasure warmed Karen's cheeks and glowed from her brown eyes. Flattered out of proportion to the simple compliment, she lowered her gaze to her plate. The meal had been good, she supposed, although she wasn't as positive as he—she'd been too aware of his presence at the table to really taste any of it. Appalled by the tremor in her fingertips, Karen raised her glass and gulped the last of her wine. Obviously remembering the night before, Paul arched his brows as he hefted the wine bottle. She smiled and nodded. He refilled her glass the instant she set it on the table again.

"We may as well finish it," he said, pouring the last of the chardonnay into his glass. Cradling the glass, Paul leaned back in his chair. He sat bolt upright again as a gust of wind rattled the panes in the long windows in the bowed alcove. The wind made a low, moaning sound as it whipped around the house. Paul frowned. "Storm brewing?"

Karen nodded. "I heard a weather report while I was finishing dinner. There's a storm moving up the coast. It could be messy."

"Messy?" Paul glanced at the windows as another blast of wind slammed into them. "In what way?"

"Thunder, lightning, rain, the possibility of sleet and/or snow. Gale warnings have been posted and high tides predicted," Karen said, repeating the forecast she'd heard earlier. "Surely you felt the temperature dropping while we were on the beach?"

Paul's eyes narrowed as he nodded. At his back, the wind turned into a low roar. "The house is secured?" he asked sharply.

Karen smiled. "Reasonably. There are a few things that need doing, but . . ." She lifted her shoulders in a helpless shrug.

"What things?" Leaning forward, Paul set his wine on the table.

"A couple of shutters on the second floor are loose," she said, annoyed. "And the storm doors must be hung."

"Why haven't these things been done?"

His imperious tone changed her annoyance to anger, and she bristled inwardly. Who did he think he was, anyway? And why was he ruining the easy camaraderie between them? Strangely hurt, but trying to control her temper, Karen replied evenly. "I called the man who does the work for me, but he has a long waiting list. I must wait my turn." A mocking smile shadowed her soft lips. "The house has withstood over a hundred years of storms. It won't blow away, I assure you."

"I didn't think it would," he retorted. Lifting his glass, he leaned back again, his attitude one of supreme indifference to the racket outside. "But I don't like leaving things unfinished." Raising his glass, Paul sipped the wine appreciatively, looking for all the world like an indolent, refined aristocrat. "I'll fix the shutters and hang the doors as soon as the storm wears itself out."

Karen stared at him in openmouthed amazement, stunned by the contrast between his appearance and his blandly voiced statement. Not even his efforts of that day had prepared her to hear him calmly offer to do the job of a handyman. "You?" she blurted out, unaware of the implied insult.

A dry smile curved his lips. "Why not?" he inquired politely. "I believe my capabilities run to a hammer and a screwdriver as well as bed-making and kitchen duty."

Karen suddenly, inexplicably, felt every bit as rattled as the windows behind him. Paul had given her a gentle but unmistakable verbal smack. She felt both ashamed and embarrassed by her rudeness. She had leaped to conclusions based only on appearances, an error she rarely made. Her fingers plucked nervously at the woven place mat beneath her plate. "I'm sorry," she murmured, glancing down and issuing a silent command to her fingers to be still. Paul's reflexes were quicker than hers. Leaning forward, he stilled her fingers by covering them with his own.

"Why are you suddenly shying away from me, Karen?" he asked, his voice so soft it felt like a caress.

Her head jerked up. "I'm not!" she said, much too forcefully, her lips burning with the memory of his brief kiss.

Paul's dark eyes met her gaze. "Yes, you are," he said. "And I know why."

She was suddenly hot, and cold, and breathless. Wanting to jump and run, but unable to move, Karen moved her head slowly back and forth, silently negating the known but unstated. She bit her lip to keep from crying out when his hand tightened around hers.

"You know why, too."

"No." Her voice was raspy, whispery, fearful. She didn't want to hear it, didn't want her feelings, her *needs*, put into words.

"Karen."

The low, aching sound of his voice shuddered through her receptive body. Her head moved again, sharply. This couldn't be happening, not to her! Not with this man! A gasped "Oh" burst from her slightly parted lips, as retaining his grip on her hand, Paul set his glass aside and got up to circle the table to her.

"Paul, don't." The whisper was nothing more than a token protest. Karen knew it, and Paul knew it, too.

"I must." Grasping her arms, he drew her up and into an embrace. "I wanted more this afternoon, Karen," he said in a tone growing harsh with passion. "I don't understand it any more than you do. But I need to taste your mouth again. I *must* have your mouth." A wildness darkened his eyes as his gaze fell on her trembling lips.

"Paul, this is crazy!" Karen's weak tone was unconvincing. "We don't know—" Her voice was lost inside his mouth.

Unlike his earlier, gentle touch, his kiss was at once hard and demanding, and his body was, too. His arms tightened, crushing her soft breasts against the muscled strength of his chest. Frightened by the intensity of the sensations searing through her, Karen struggled against his hold. She went still as his tongue entered her mouth. Her senses reeling, she felt his hands move on her back, one up to her head, fingers tangling in her hair, the other to the base of her spine, fingers splaying over her buttocks. She felt him change position. One leg eased between her thighs and was immediately followed by the other. The pressure stretched the denim material of her skirt, molding it to the most feminine part of her. Cupping his hand, he drew her up and into the shocking heat of his body.

"Paul!" she gasped, tearing her mouth from his. "You must stop!" Karen could feel his heart thumping against her chest, could hear the erratic sound of his harsh breath, could smell the dizzying mixture of sharp after-shave and aroused male. He frightened her; he excited her. She felt as if her insides were melting.

"I know," he said unsteadily. Drawing deep gulps of air into his lungs, he rested his forehead against hers, but his hand continued to press her body to his. "I feel you trembling," he said on a roughly expelled breath that teased her lips. "I don't want to frighten you, Karen. Please believe that."

"I . . . I do." Karen was telling the truth; she did believe him. The strain in his voice convinced her that he was as confused as she was by the intensity of the attraction flaring between them. Held rigidly at her sides, her hands ached with the need to touch him, caress him, hold him. She clenched her fingers in desperation. "Please, let me go." Karen's throat felt tight and achy. "I must clear the table." She was half hoping he'd refuse, and she sighed softly when he complied.

Paul reluctantly slid his hands from her body, then stepped back, a wry smile slanting his lips. "Do you want me to leave?"

"Now, tonight?" Karen exclaimed, her jangled senses clamoring a protest. "There's a storm building out there!" As if to reinforce her statement, a gust of wind slammed against the house. "Where would you go?" Glancing away from the passion still smoldering in his eyes, Karen stared into the darkness beyond the windows. She didn't want him to leave, and it required all her control to keep from clutching him to her. She started when his hand caught her chin, turning her to face him.

"You didn't answer my question, Karen," he said tightly. "Do you *want* me to go?"

Unconscious of the implied sensuousness of her act, Karen moistened her dry lips with the tip of her tongue, shivering at the naked hunger revealed in his eyes as he watched her. Thrown off balance by the intensity of her response to him, she jerked around and began clattering dishes and utensils as she gathered them together.

"Answer me!"

The sharpness of his tone lashed at her, and with a muffled sob, Karen whipped around to look at him. "No!" she shouted. "No, I don't want you to go!" Gripping the dishes in her hands, she spun on her heel and dashed into the kitchen, wincing at the harsh sound of his voice as Paul cursed fluently.

Dammit! Dammit! Dammit! Feeling about to explode, Paul stormed into the living room. A fire leaped merrily in the fireplace, sending forth a rosy light to enhance the welcoming comfort of the room. Paul wasn't soothed by the warmth of the fire or the appeal of the deeply cushioned chintz-covered chairs and sofa, the brightly colored braided oval rug or the glow from the softly burnished copper lamps set on the solid wood tables. If anything, the tranquil ambience of the room merely added irritation to his already abraded sensibilities. Flinging his body into a chair, he stared broodingly into the crackling flames.

Why had it happened, here and now? Paul asked himself agitatedly. More to the point, *how* had it happened? A burst of dry, humorless laughter eased the tension in his throat. Had he genuinely believed that his sex life was a thing of the past? Yes, he had convinced himself that the drive was gone forever.

"Fool!"

The ridicule wrapped up in the sound of his own voice brought a self-mocking smile to Paul's lips. Impotence. Merely allowing the word to form instilled a sense of sick dread in him. But he had believed it to be true. For six years, Paul had lived with the feeling of dread. Six long years. Sighing softly, tiredly, he rested his head against the back of the chair and closed his eyes.

More than six years earlier, in the classic last-to-know fashion, he had learned of his wife's infidelities and her proclivity for younger men—compliments of a well-meaning friend. At the time, something had seemed to die inside Paul. His body had not responded to either his wife or any other member of the opposite sex since then. At first, his lack of response had terrified him, yet pride had kept him from seeking medical advice. Then, as time passed and his interest waned, Paul had resigned himself to never again experiencing the sensual thrill of his blood running hot and wild and his body tautening in anticipation. And now, after six years, to have his body awaken to urgent, pulsating life, not once but repeatedly within a matter of some twenty-four hours, was stupefying, to say the least.

Not repeatedly, incessantly, Paul thought wryly, feeling his muscles tense and the sweet flame of desire sear his loins as a vision of Karen came into his mind.

What was it about her? Shaking his head, Paul dismissed the question as unimportant. The why of it didn't matter—not now. What did matter was the life and passion quickening his body and teasing his mind. He wanted her. His desire was strong and hot, and he wanted her so much it actually caused him pain. God, it was wonderful!

"Where is your wife?"

His sensual reverie shattered by Karen's quiet voice, Paul shot up in the chair. His mind still clouded by a haze of passion, he stared at her uncomprehendingly.

"My wife?" he repeated blankly.

Karen's lips tightened. "Yes," she said distinctly. "Your wife." Her steps light, her walk graceful, she crossed the room to stand before him. Her gaze was cool and direct. "Where is she now?"

A flash of understanding removed the frown creasing Paul's brow. He had told her he was both a father and a grandfather, but that was all he'd told her. And after the trauma of her revelations the night before, they had both carefully avoided any subject even bordering on the personal all day. They had talked of many things, all of them impersonal. But now, Paul realized that Karen needed answers—she believed him married and looking for some extramarital action. And considering her own experience with Charles, she was probably somewhat militant, and rightfully so. A slight smile teased Paul's lips. No wonder she was looking at him in that insulted, accusatory way.

"My wife is dead, Karen," he said, rising to stand in front of her. "She's been dead for almost seven months."

"I'm sorry." Her lashes swept down to conceal her eyes, but not quite fast enough to hide the flash of relief that they revealed.

Reaching out, he caught her hand with his. "You needn't be," he murmured, feeling heat shoot up his arm as he stroked his thumb over the back of her hand. "She had been on a course of self-destruction for years."

Karen started, and her lashes swept up again. "You mean she committed suicide?" she breathed.

"No." Paul shook his head sharply. "At least not consciously. It's a long, unsavory story, and..." His voice faded. He couldn't simply say "...and I'd rather make love to you than talk about her now."

"I'm sorry," she repeated.

"Don't be." Paul was hurting again and enjoying every nuance of physical pain. Lifting her hand, he brought it to his lips. His tongue tested the tips of her fingers and found them delicious. "She was driven by demons no one understood. She's at peace now." As he finished speaking, he drew one finger into his mouth to suck gently on the tip. Satisfaction shimmered through him when Karen gasped, then shivered.

"Paul." Her voice was low, quivery. "What are you doing?"

"Tasting you." A slow smile curved his lips. "You taste like lemon-fresh dish detergent."

"I...I had to wash the broiler. It doesn't fit in the dishwasher."

Paul's smile deepened. Karen's tone was revealing in its uncertainty. "I find I'm developing a taste for the tartness of lemons," he said, deserting the finger and drawing her hand to his shoulder. "But I still prefer the sweetness of your mouth." His objective stated, Paul slowly lowered his head, allowing her time to retreat if she wanted to. She didn't.

Desire surged through Paul's body as Karen lifted her head, silently offering her mouth to him. He groaned and covered her mouth with his parted lips.

This time his kiss was different; the difference destroyed the last of Karen's resistance. Though his lips were as hard as before, his mouth was gentle on hers, coaxing a response from her. Murmuring words she couldn't hear but understood nonetheless, he played a sensual game with her lips, nipping at them and sucking on them in turn, then lightly skimming his tongue over her sensitized skin.

When Paul finally slid his tongue into her mouth, Karen had been reduced to a whimpering, shivering mass of receptive readiness. Her muffled moan of pleasure electrified him. Gentleness gave way to spiraling hunger. The kiss became an almost violent clash of greedy mouths, each seemingly intent on devouring the other.

Circling her hips with one arm, Paul pulled her into intimate contact with his body. His right hand captured one breast, fingers teasing the crest into tight, aching arousal. Karen shuddered in reaction to the pleasure splintering throughout her body. Her mind whirled. Her senses exploded. Her empty body throbbed a demand for fulfillment. A low moan of protest burst from her throat when he deserted her mouth to seek her ear with his lips.

"Come to bed with me." Paul's voice was harsh with strain, his breath hot, his body rigid.

It was sheer madness, and Karen eagerly divorced sanity. Arching her body into his, she closed her eyes and let her head fall back, exposing the vulnerable cords in her neck to his voracious mouth.

"Karen. Karen." Paul wrenched a moan from her as he drew the moist tip of his tongue down her throat to her fluttering pulse. "Come to bed with me." The touch of his tongue whipped her pulse beat into thunder. The noise created by nature outside paled by comparison.

Consumed by an intensity of passion she had never before experienced, Karen was oblivious to any and all outside influences. The force of the worsening storm battering the house went unheard by her, as did the spit and crackle of the dying fire in the grate. She herself was a living flame contained within a raging storm; the blaze was beautiful.

"Karen?" Paul brought his hands up to grasp her head, making her look at him as he stared at her with eyes lit from within by the desire running rampant through his body. "We need each other tonight." His raw voice revealed the fine edge he was teetering on. "Say yes."

"Yes."

Paul went absolutely still for an instant, not even seeming to breathe. Then a fine tremor rippled through his body. His voice was little more than an aching whisper.

"Where?"

The time for hesitation was long past. Having accepted the idea of going to bed with him, Karen moved swiftly to consummate her commitment.

"My room," she said, grasping his hand as she whirled away, heading for the stairs.

They ran. Hands clasped, they dashed up the stairs, along the hall and into Karen's bedroom. The door stood wide open behind them; in their haste, neither Karen nor Paul noticed.

Between quick, hard kisses and brief, eager touches, they literally tore the clothes from one another's backs. Paul dragged Karen into a crushing embrace the instant they were free of the confining material. The mat of hair on his chest scraped her breasts into tingling arousal. Her soft curves yielded to his tightly bunched muscles. His mouth was hot; her lips were parted and ready for his.

Denied the food of love for such a long time, their bodies were starving, his to fill, hers to be filled. Their hands moved restlessly in unison, stroking, kneading, caressing. Their bodies strained as if to absorb and be absorbed, one into the other.

"Not enough, it's not enough," Paul groaned into her mouth, moving her inexorably toward the bed. "I want more. I want everything."

"Yes. Yes." Karen's senses swam as he bore her back onto the bed. "Now, please," she sobbed, grasping his hips as he moved between her thighs.

He could not hold back, and she didn't want him to. Communicating her desire by pressing her fingers into his taut buttocks, she raised her hips as he thrust his forward. A cry of exquisite pleasure was torn from her arched throat as his body surged into hers, making them one.

Karen did not hold back—she could not, not even the small, inhibited portion of herself that she had never been able to allow her husband to own. Feeling stronger, more vital, more alive than she'd ever felt in her life, Karen abandoned herself to the sensual fury of Paul's driving possession. He had demanded everything; her body granted his demand.

"Yes, like that," he groaned as she curled her legs around him in a lover's embrace. "Hold me close, tighter, tighter."

"Oh, Paul, yes!" she cried, arching her back as he drew her breast into his mouth.

"Lord! I want more and more," he gasped, grasping her hips to lift her up and into his cadence. "I can't get enough of you!"

"Paul. Paul!" Karen gave a low-pitched scream as his momentum drove her over the edge of reason and into the realm of shattering, pulsating release.

"Oh, God! Karen!" Paul's harsh cry of triumph echoed through the silent room a moment later.

Karen awoke to the chill sound of sleet being flung against the windows by a wind howling in rage and the warm feeling of a broad palm stroking her thigh. Reacting to both sound and sensation, she murmured appreciatively and moved toward the source of the warmth. Paul's skin was heated, his body aroused.

"I want you again," he whispered, brushing his lips along her jawline to her ear, then over her cheek to the corner of her mouth.

"I know." Turning her head, Karen returned the caress by gliding her lips over the taut skin on his face.

"For purely scientific reasons, you understand." Amusement underlined his serious tone.

"Indeed?" Karen's lips quirked into a smile. "Name one."

"Well, there's the obvious, of course."

"And that is?" Her smile deepened.

"Sweet lady, I'm over fifty, remember?" Paul's tone held a suspicious hint of self-satisfaction. "It'll be worth the experiment just to find out if I *can*."

As she could feel the strength pressing against her thigh that assured her he *could*, Karen laughed softly. "Name another," she insisted, catching his lower lip carefully between her teeth.

"I have a scientist's curiosity to find out if you're really as good as I thought you were or if I was just that anxious."

Amused and challenged at the same time, Karen pulled away from him and sat up. "You thought I was good?" Reaching across the bed, she switched on the small lamp on the nightstand, wanting to see his expression when he answered. He quickly hid a twitching smile when she turned back to him.

"Well, yes, as I said, I *thought* you were good." Paul's tone was suspiciously bland. "But, as I also admitted, I *was* anxious and therefore not very objective."

"I see." Actually, Karen saw more than was good for her equilibrium. Paul was lying flat on his back, his torso bathed by the soft golden lamplight. Silver glinted in the dark hair at his temples and in the curly mat on his chest. Fascinated by the silver strands, Karen wondered if they grew in the line of darkness that ran from his chest across his midriff and under the sheet draping his concave abdomen.

"What do you . . . see?" Paul's tone tightened perceptibly as he watched her eyes widen slightly as her gaze settled on the sheet.

"Uh...um...what?" Karen jerked around to look at him. The sudden movement set her bare breasts swaying, making her aware of her nudity for the first time since she'd sat up. Dismayed by her impulse to cross her arms over her chest, she straightened her spine and looked at him with hard-won composure.

Her effort was wasted on Paul; he was too engrossed in staring at her breasts to notice. Warmth suffused Karen's body as he slowly lifted his hand from the bed to gently, tentatively touch one quivering tip with one finger.

"Beautiful," he whispered, lightly stroking the crest to aching attention.

"Is, uh . . ." Karen was finding it extremely difficult to sit still. "Is this part of the experiment?" she asked, swallowing to ease the sudden dryness in her throat. Paul smiled as his stroking finger wrenched an involuntary gasp from her lips.

"This *is* the experiment," he said, raising his shadowed eyes to hers. "Although I readily admit to being overanxious," he murmured, transferring his finger to give equal consideration to her other breast. "I've reached the conclusion you are an exceptionally good bed partner."

A sexist remark if Karen had ever heard one, yet instead of feeling insulted or annoyed by it, she felt ridiculously complimented and pleased. She also felt an urge to lean forward to grasp his hand and bring it to her. Her breasts hurt and felt heavy. She silently willed him to cradle their weight in his palms. The pad of his finger continued its maddening stroke.

"Paul?" His name barely whispered from her tight throat.

"Yes?" His voice was low and raw. His finger flicked, igniting a blast of sensation that Karen felt in the depths of her femininity.

"You're driving me crazy!" she gasped, shuddering.

"What are you gonna do about it?"

Karen gazed at him in astonishment. Taunting challenge gleamed in his dark eyes. Indecision held her motionless for a long moment. Claiming exclusive rights to the role of conqueror, Karen's former husband had never allowed her to play the aggressor. Paul was not allowing it, either; he was demanding it. An unfurling flame of excitement consumed her last lingering shred of inhibition. Accepting his challenge, she coiled her fingers around his wrists and drew his palms to her breasts. A satisfied smile tilted the corners of Paul's lips. Moving slowly, she pressed her body against his hands as she lowered her head to his chest. Paul's smile fled, and he inhaled sharply as she curled her tongue around one tight bud nestled in the silver-and-black mat on his chest.

Paul's fingers flexed in reaction to her caress. "More, please," he groaned, gently kneading her soft flesh. "I love the feel of your mouth and hands on my body." To reinforce his claim, he moved one hand to the back of her head and speared his fingers through her hair.

As she nuzzled into the salt-and-pepper curls, Karen's senses were assailed by the heady scent of soap and musk. Her tongue tingled with the slightly salty taste of his skin. Feeling free, unfettered, she explored his chest leisurely before gliding her lips down the slight incline from his rib cage to his navel. Paul's fingers gripped her hair spasmodically as she dipped her tongue into the shallow indentation. His body jerked when her moist lips continued to follow the dark, downy trail.

"Karen!" Paul grasped her shoulders, halting her lips mere inches from their destination. "I can't take any more. I want to be inside you."

Karen gave him a dry look.

"I appreciate the thought, and I'll probably beg you for it some other time." His smile was rakish with promise as he pulled her on top of him.

Karen gasped; the unique position held appeal, exciting appeal. Straightening, she stared into his eyes, thrilling to the taut expectancy that flashed in their depths as she carefully straddled his hard thighs. His hands grasped her hips. Their gazes dropped to watch as she lowered her body, sheathing him deep inside her silken warmth.

"That's good," he groaned, arching up into her. "So good."

"Yes," Karen sighed, quivering as his hands sought her breasts. "I never knew anything could feel this good." Her breath lodged in her throat as he thrust upward again. She began to move responsively.

"Slowly, slowly," Paul crooned in a hoarse tone. "I want to savor every minute of it."

Releasing her breasts, Paul reached up to cup her face with his palms and draw her mouth to his. While she rocked against him, his tongue reflected the slow thrust-and-retreat motion of his body. His hands slid down her neck to her shoulders. Stroking, caressing, he glided his palms down her body to where their separate beings were joined into one.

Karen's breathing was shallow and then deep by turns. Inside she felt like a time bomb about to run out of seconds. She was trying to maintain the slow pace Paul wanted, but it was becoming more and more difficult to hold herself in check. White lightning zigzagged through her when she felt him work his fingers between their fused bodies.

"Now, Karen," he cried, suddenly increasing his thrusting cadence. "Now!"

She was moving wildly, gasping his name, when the last second ticked and her inner bomb exploded, flinging her into a whirlpool of ecstatic exhaustion.

Chapter Four

A persistent rapping sound finally succeeded in piercing to the depths of the most restful slumber Karen had enjoyed in years. Prying her eyes to half-mast, she lay listening to the regular beat, eyebrows meeting in a frown as she tried to identify the cause and location of the disturbance. The noise ceased and her expression eased, only to tighten again when the rapping resumed.

"What the—" muttering, Karen tossed back the tangled covers and swung her legs over the side of the bed to sit up. A twinge of complaint in her thighs brought memories of the night before rushing into her mind. Blinking once, she scooted around to stare at the empty bed. Heat flooded her face as vivid images of the nocturnal activity played out upon the rumpled sheets flashed through her suddenly cleared brain.

Where was Paul?

Thinking his name brought his image to her mind and a deeper flush to her cheeks. Had she really caressed him, kissed him and then— Moaning softly, Karen fell back onto the mattress, at once embarrassed by her actions and hopeful of an opportunity to repeat them.

Heat suffusing her body, Karen curled into a tight ball. Her throat felt thick and clogged. Her body felt heavy and overly warm. Her emotions felt battered and her mind was sluggish. Separate threads, one of shame, the other of anticipation, tangled inside her, tying her entire nervous system into knots.

Like pulsating impulses, individual and distinct scenes flashed in her memory, making her hot and cold by turns. Moaning softly, Karen buried her face in the pillow. A half sigh, half sob rose to choke her as she inhaled the scent that her mind would forever connect exclusively with Paul.

As her mind formed his name, her throat expelled the choking sob.

What had come over her? Karen asked herself, her thoughts scattering as her mind sought reasons—or excuses—for her uncharacteristic behavior. Never, not even with the man she had married and believed herself deeply in love with, had she so abandoned herself while in the throes of lovemaking. It simply wasn't like her. And since her divorce she had not experienced the slightest desire for a man, any man. Yet she had responded wildly to Paul.

What must he be thinking about her now, in the light of morning? Karen wondered, blanching at the thought. If upon awakening Paul had labeled her a wanton woman, she had given him ample reason to do so. She had behaved wantonly!

But then, Paul had behaved like the male equivalent of a wanton, whatever that might be.

The realization that she and Paul had in fact been perfectly matched in bed resolved the emotional upheaval. The sense of shame subsided, overcome by a sense of anticipation. Uncurling slowly, Karen raised her arms and stretched languorously.

There was a stirring deep inside Karen's body, a tingling response to her memories and thoughts of Paul. She wanted him again; it was as simple and basic as that. With realization came resolution. She had never allowed herself personal indulgence. Raised to work hard and apply herself conscientiously, she had always done the "right" thing. She had been a virgin when she married; she had known no other man but her husband. She was no longer an idealistic, wide-eyed young girl; she no longer expected the world or her own niche in it to be perfect. She was getting uncomfortably close to forty and lately had begun to feel vaguely that life was slipping through her fingers, not unlike the sands in an hourglass. Surely every individual was to be allowed one step off the straight and narrow? Karen asked herself. Her lips twisted in bitter remembrance.

Her former husband had spent more time dancing off the straight and narrow than walking on it. *He* had not paid the price of loneliness and uncertainty about encroaching middle age! Why then should she? Karen demanded silently. She was her own person, a free adult, fully capable of making her own decisions. Should she feel shame and remorse because her senses had rejoiced in the act of giving her body in sweetly satisfying abandonment?

No! The cry of denial rang inside Karen's head. Paul had not taken her, nor had he used her. Rather, Paul had shared with her the beauty of exquisite pleasure given and received. And, though she and Paul were strangers, they were also lovers. Karen had no idea how long her lover would stay with her. But then, did anyone ever know what the future held? The question darkened Karen's eyes with remembered pain. In the final analysis, she had been forced to acknowledge that the man she had loved, married and created children with was a stranger to her. And she had given that man everything of herself. She had only given her body to Paul. As the mist of pain cleared from her eyes, Karen decided she could live with the knowledge of her gift to him.

She had behaved wantonly—and she had loved every second of it! A slow smile curving her lips, Karen stretched again, sinuously. She felt wonderful—no, she felt much, much more than merely wonderful. She felt beautiful, and she had never before felt beautiful. She felt bone-deep satisfaction, and she had never before experienced that feeling, either. But most of all she felt as though she had not been expertly loved but exquisitely cherished, and that feeling warmed her inside and out. And the perpetrator of every one of her delicious feelings was not only a man she barely knew but a fantastic, excitingly virile man who, in his own words, would never see fifty again!

Where was Paul, anyway? Frowning again, Karen absently smoothed her hands over the spot where he had lain and sank into the memory of Paul's fiercely gentle possession. She felt quite certain she could happily laze the day away in dreamy expectation of the coming night—if it weren't for that annoying rapping noise, which had resumed after a long pause of blessed quiet.

The sound intruded, breaking the spell. Sighing, Karen left the bed, deciding she might as well get dressed and investigate. If she had any luck at all, the racket was being caused by Gil Rawlins, the handyman she'd called to prepare the house for winter.

Some twenty-odd minutes later, showered and dressed in her usual workday attire of faded jeans and a sweatshirt, Karen was stripping the sheets from the bed when the hammering, which had ceased once more while she was in the bathroom, commenced outside her bedroom window. Tossing the linens to the floor, she walked to the window and opened it. A welcoming smile on her lips, she stuck her head through the opening to call a greeting to Gil.

The man poised on the ladder, busily hammering nails into the shutter hinges, in no way resembled the short, stocky Gil Rawlins. This man was lean and muscular, and the physical work he was engaged in was at odds with his elegant appearance.

"Paul?" Incredulity lent a hollow note to Karen's voice. "What in the world do you think you're doing?"

The hammer paused in midswing. Paul slanted a smile at her before following through. "Good morning to you, too." The hammer made contact with a resounding bang. Paul relaxed against the ladder with negligent ease. "And I don't *think* I'm doing anything—I *am* fixing the shutters." His smile widened.

"In fact," he continued, indicating his work with a motion of his head, "this is the last of the lot. I'll be finished shortly."

"Finished?" Karen frowned. "How long have you been at it?"

"Since first light." He grinned at her look of astonishment. "I'm a creature of habit, and I always wake at dawn." His grin grew decidedly suggestive. "Regardless of how, ah, active my night happened to be."

Karen felt a sting of color on her cheeks that had absolutely nothing to do with the sharpness of the tangy sea breeze. Feeling unequal to the rakish gleam brightening his dark eyes, she lowered her glance.

"Did you, er—" she paused to clear her suddenly dry throat "—have you eaten anything?" Karen glanced up to catch a tender smile curving his lips.

"No." He shook his head and arched one dark eyebrow. "Are you offering to cook me breakfast?"

"Well, the sign out by the road does advertise bed *and* breakfast."

"I seem to recall dinner, as well." Paul's tone was low, shaded sensuously by the memory of the bed that had followed rather than preceded the meal.

The warmth in Karen's cheeks intensified. Her voice was low and tinged with uncertainty. "Since you're the only guest, I—I decided to include lunch and dinner in the reduced fall room rate."

"I'll try to earn my meals." Though Paul's tone was somber, his eyes gleamed with devilry.

He had certainly earned his breakfast!

Karen's face flamed as the thought flashed into her head. As if he could actually read her mind, Paul burst out laughing and nearly lost his precarious perch on the ladder. With a muffled exclamation, he grabbed for the windowsill and caught Karen's hand. His position once again reasonably secure, Paul grinned into her frightened eyes.

"Unless you want a severely injured guest on your hands," he said, still grinning, "I suggest you withdraw from this window and let me get on with the work." Moving carefully, he shifted his hand to the sill alongside hers.

"Are you sure you'll be all right?" Karen frowned with concern.

"I was doing fine until you popped your head out and distracted me." As he stared into her anxious eyes, Paul's grin slowly faded. "Karen," he said in a low, chiding voice, "I am not the complete dilettante. I assure you I will be fine." He paused an instant, then continued even as she began to protest, "Unless, of course, I starve to death first."

"Paul—"

"Go," he ordered, hefting the hammer. "I'll be finished in a few minutes."

Wanting to argue but deciding she'd better not, Karen withdrew her head and closed the window. Gathering up the bundle of laundry, she left the bedroom and went downstairs, half expecting to hear a cry followed by a crash.

His expression pensive, Paul ignored the cold sea wind biting at every inch of exposed skin on his body and stared at the windowpane that reflected the sparkling sunlight.

Had he come on too strong? he mused. His lips curved in self-derision. Yes, of course he'd come on too strong; he had been coming on to Karen much too strongly from the beginning. He was, in fact, behaving like a wild-eyed pubescent boy subservient to his hormones.

But damn, Karen did have the strangest effect on him! Paul's smile acquired a sensuous tilt. Gripping the hammer in his right hand, he slammed a nail into the shutter hinge with commendable accuracy. The similarity between the act and his performance the night before was not lost on Paul. Without warning, his body tightened and the muscles in his thighs quivered with taut readiness. Laughing aloud from the sheer joy of the almost painful arousal, Paul hammered another nail home.

Okay, he had come on too strong, and much too soon, Paul admitted to himself. But Karen had responded so warmly, so sweetly, and it had been so long, so very long since he'd felt even the most minute twinge of need for a woman's warmth and sweetness, that he could not dredge up a hint of regret for his impetuosity.

Paul let his arm drop to his side. The hammer and the shutter, indeed even his precarious position on the ladder, were momentarily forgotten. Closing his eyes, he savored the revived heat of passion rushing through his body.

Lord, it felt good to experience the life quickening his body after nearly six years of feeling dead sensually. Relishing the tightness in his loins, Paul opened his eyes, tossed back his head and laughed into the chill autumn breeze. He felt young and strong and equal to anything life had to offer. He wanted to make love to Karen all day and then all night.

But first . . . Paul laughed again. First he had to finish repairing the shutters. The hammer struck the nail with a resounding bang.

Although she strained to hear the slightest sound as she loaded the washer before hurrying into the kitchen to start breakfast, Karen's fears for Paul went unrealized.

Tension coiled within her as she automatically prepared the meal. Paul should be making an appearance in the kitchen at any moment. What could she say to him? Karen swallowed around a tight knot forming in her throat. Feeling awkward and inept, she overbeat the eggs and clattered the cutlery as she set the table. The eggs she'd scrambled were ready to be served when Paul sauntered into the kitchen. Coming to a stop near the sink, he struck an elegant pose and held his arms out.

"There, you see? I'm still in one piece."

"I'm sorry."

"That I'm still in one piece?"

"No, of course not!" Karen frowned at his teasing smile. "I'm sorry about insulting your capabilities."

Paul's smile turned wry. "It wasn't so much my capabilities that were insulted as much as my intelligence," he informed her in a dry tone. He didn't notice her deepening frown as he turned to the sink to wash his dusty hands.

Karen mulled over his words as she filled two plates with the steaming food and carried them to the table. "Will you bring the toast?" she asked, indicating the breadbasket on the countertop with a distracted motion of her head.

"Certainly." Eyeing her narrowly, Paul picked up the linen-covered basket and strolled to the table. "What's the problem?" He raised one brow as he sat down opposite her.

"I'm not sure I understand," she confessed, frowning at the stream of coffee she was pouring into his cup.

"Understand what?" Paul asked, his knife poised over the sausage nestled next to the home-fried potatoes on his plate.

Karen finished filling her own cup with the aromatic coffee before glancing up at him. "I'm not sure I understand exactly how I've insulted your intelligence."

"Oh." Enlightenment brought a tiny smile to his lips. "It's quite basic, really." Paul's shoulders moved in a half shrug. "Any person with a modicum of intelligence can perform almost any task. All that's required is a willingness to do the work and application of common sense." He smiled. "And although I'll readily admit that my life's work was not of the physical variety, I do consider myself a reasonably intelligent person, and fastening shutter hinges hardly requires all that much brain- or muscle-power." He smiled slightly. "Now do you understand?"

"Oh, yes, I understand now." Karen didn't return his smile. Inside she was simmering. What a condescending son of a— Fortunately, Paul interrupted her thoughts before she blurted them aloud.

"Since I was only teasing to begin with, it's really unimportant, anyway."

Karen blinked. "You were teasing?"

"Yes, of course." Paul smiled wryly. "Karen, I face myself in a mirror every day. I know exactly how I look."

"Look?" she repeated blankly, so confused she forgot her feeling of awkwardness. "I'm afraid you've lost me."

"I'm a banker, and I look it," he said, his voice flat with self-knowledge. He raised one hand for her inspection; it was not the hand of a day laborer. The fingernails were short, blunt and clean, as was the entire hand. Karen couldn't detect a hint of callus on his palm. "Hardly the hand of a man accustomed to hard physical work, is it?"

"No." Karen frowned. "So what?" She had never been enthralled by dirty fingernails and rough calluses.

"So I fully understood your skepticism concerning my capabilities with a hammer, let alone a ladder." Paul's gentle smile contradicted the savage knife thrust he made into the innocent sausage.

"It bothers you!" she exclaimed, astounded by the realization.

"It never did before, but lately, yes, it bothers me."

"Why?" Karen stared at him, her breakfast forgotten. Her eyes revealing the confusion she felt, she slowly lowered her gaze to the upper half of his body. Though slender, Paul was by no stretch of the imagination spare. His chest and shoulders were not those of a professional athlete but were broad enough to draw admiring glances. He was muscular without appearing overdeveloped. Mr. America he wasn't, and thank heaven for that, Karen thought, smiling as she lifted her gaze to his slightly narrowed eyes. "There's nothing wrong with the way you look," she declared in a tone of utter conviction.

"Thank you." A flush tinted the taut skin over Paul's high cheekbones. "But if that's true, why were you so amazed to discover me repairing the shutters?" His dark eyes gleamed challengingly.

"You didn't answer my question about why the way you look bothers you," Karen said evasively.

Paul slanted an arch look at her. "Ladies first," he insisted in a teasing tone.

Suddenly impatient with the discussion, Karen swept his torso with a cool, calculating glance. "Okay, I'll confess," she said, meeting his gaze. "You have the appearance of a born-with-the-silver-spoon aristocrat. There's an aura of breeding and elegance about you that conflicts with the idea of any kind of physical labor. Not that you look incapable of labor—it's just that you've never had to perform it. And that's why I was surprised to find you repairing the shutters."

"I see." His breakfast forgotten, Paul stared at her for a few tense moments. Then a smile twitched his sculpted male lips. "An aura of elegance, hmm?" He arched one dark eyebrow very effectively. Karen gave way to a grin.

"Yes. A definite aura of elegance."

"You find this, er... *aura* attractive?"

Karen's grin curved into a wry smile. "I always believed that actions speak louder than words," she murmured, obliquely referring to her eager response to him the night before.

"You were satisfied with my nocturnal labor?"

A warm flush began at the base of Karen's throat and crept upward to her cheeks. Yet, even flustered, she caught the hint of uncertainty in Paul's tone. Could he possibly harbor doubts about his own prowess? she wondered, examining him more closely.

Paul's expression could only be described as austere, but there was a tenseness about him, as if...Karen searched her mind for a fitting phrase that would define the emotion she sensed emanating from him. Then it hit her. It was as if he was waiting for a life-or-death verdict to be handed down!

Forgetting her embarrassment, Karen obeyed an impulse to reach across the table and slide her hand over his. "Yes, Paul, I was satisfied, deeply satisfied," she admitted in a soft, steady voice.

The slow movement of Paul's chest revealed the soundless sigh he expelled. "So was I," he said, turning his hand to glide his palm against hers. "I was deeply satisfied in more ways than you can imagine."

Karen was both intrigued and confused by his cryptic statement. Satisfied in more ways? she repeated to herself. What— The forming question was washed from her mind by a flood of sensations activated by the feel of his fingers lacing with hers. Biting back an exclamation of pleasure, she raised her gaze to his darkening eyes.

"Paul?"

"I want very much to experience the satisfaction again." His voice was low and warm and fantastically sexy. Excitement warring with trepidation inside her, Karen blurted out the first thought that jumped into her mind.

"But we haven't even finished breakfast!"

"Karen..." Paul's voice dropped to a crooning, heated whisper. "The hunger clawing at me cannot be appeased by food." Lifting her hand, he bent to brush his lips across her fingers, and Karen felt the heat from his mouth in every nerve ending in her body.

"It's...it's morning!" Karen's voice was reedy, her breathing uneven.

"Yes." Paul's lips explored her knuckles.

"The sun's shining!"

"Yes." His tongue slid provocatively between her fingers.

"Paul." His name sighed through her slightly parted lips.

"I want to be with you, a part of you, now, in the morning, and here, in the sunshine."

Karen surrendered, simply because she wanted to. "Yes."

Retaining his hold on her hand, Paul stood and moved around the table to her. Smiling into her widened eyes, he dropped to his knees. With a gentle tug, he drew her down next to him. Moving carefully, as if she were constructed of the most delicate spun glass, he lowered her to the carpet. Looming over her, he captured her gaze with his dark eyes and the hem of her sweatshirt with his fingers. Swiftly, smoothly, he drew the shirt from her body, exposing her unfettered breasts to his heated gaze. A shiver rocketed the length of her spine as he lowered his head to her breasts.

"Paul. Oh, Paul!" Karen cried his name huskily, twisting and arching her back in response to the pleasure he created by flicking his tongue over one tingling crest. As his lips closed around the aroused peak, his hands slid to the snap on her jeans.

"Help me." Paul's voice held an enchanting mixture of plea and command as he released the zipper and tugged on her jeans.

Helpless against the sensuous excitement rushing through her body, Karen kicked the loafers from her feet and lifted her hips from the carpet. In the next instant she was naked and vulnerable to Paul's eyes and touch. But within moments she was not alone in her vulnerability. Pushing upright, Paul literally tore the clothes from his body. Noticing her smoky-eyed gaze, he stood over her, quivering as she examined him.

Karen stared at his tall form with fascinated curiosity. In the unforgiving light of day, Paul's body was even more appealing than when cloaked by darkness. His well-muscled shoulders and chest tapered to a flat abdomen and narrow hips. His lightly haired legs were long and well formed. And, in full arousal, he presented a breathtaking image of the primal male. And the primal male excited the primitive female inside Karen. Obeying a life drive as old as time, she opened her arms in silent invitation.

"Karen." Paul groaned as he dropped to his knees between her thighs. "You don't know," he murmured tightly, grasping her hips to lift her to him. "You can't possibly know..." His words were drowned by the harsh breath he inhaled as he joined his body with hers.

For an instant, Karen was confused, wondering what he had started to say. Then it no longer mattered; nothing mattered but the spiraling tension luring her toward the edge of reason.

* * *

Paul's chest felt constricted from lack of air. His entire body felt tightly wired, and he held on to the last of his control with grim determination. Beneath him, Karen twisted and arched and whimpered his name; her panting voice was the sweetest sound he had ever heard. Never had a woman, any woman, responded to him so freely or given herself to him so completely. In these few moments of possession, Karen was his in an incomprehensible way that transcended the merely physical. In an effort to maintain that exquisite if inexplicable sense of ownership, Paul fought to contain the fire of desire consuming his mind and body. He would pleasure Karen before he sought his own ecstatic release.

Paul was hovering on the brink of sensual discovery, gritting his teeth, when Karen gave herself to soaring completion. Buried deeply in her warmth, holding her tightly to him, Paul shuddered, then followed her over the edge of reason.

He didn't want to move. As his breathing returned to normal, Paul decided he could happily spend the rest of his life as he was at that moment: his body still joined with Karen's, his head pillowed on her soft breasts.

It was not be be. The phone rang.

"I must answer it," Karen said softly.

"Why?"

"It's one of my quirks," she confessed, pushing against his chest. "I can't stand not answering a ringing phone."

Paul sighed but moved to untangle their bodies, stretching out on the carpet beside her. The instant she was free, Karen scrambled to her feet.

"Aren't you going to dress?" she asked, scooping her clothing from the floor before heading toward the kitchen and the shrilling wall phone.

"Eventually," Paul murmured, stretching.

Clutching her rumpled garments to her chest with one hand, Karen reached for the receiver with her other hand and turned to glance back at Paul. His long body lay sprawled in a patch of bright morning sunlight. His eyes were closed. A tiny smile of satisfaction curved his lips. At that moment, Karen wanted nothing more than to ignore the persistently ringing phone and run into the dining alcove to cuddle next to him on the floor.

Indecision held her hand motionless in midair for a moment. Then, sighing softly, she grasped the receiver and brought it to her ear.

"Hello?" she said with barely concealed impatience.

"Karen?"

Karen frowned as she identified the anxious strain in the voice of her former mother-in-law. "Yes. Judith?" Her frown deepened. "Is something wrong?" Immediately after asking, she thought of her boys, who were in prep school in Vermont. Panic tightened her throat at the muffled sound of a sob at the other end of the line. "Judith, what is it?"

"Karen, it's Charles. He's had a heart attack!"

Charles? Karen's mind went blank for a moment. Charles was not yet forty years old! "When?" She had to push the word past her frozen lips.

"Late last night. I've been with him since he was admitted to the hospital." Judith paused for breath. "Karen, he's asking for you and the boys. Will you come?"

Karen's gaze flew to the man basking naked in the morning sunlight. *Paul.* Pain streaked through her mind and her heart. While she and Paul had been together, Charles had been fighting for his life. Shame and defeat decided the issue.

"Yes, Judith, of course I'll come. I'll be there as soon as possible."

Raising her eyes, Karen found her gaze captured and held by Paul's steady regard.

Chapter Five

Staring into Paul's eyes, Karen heard herself respond distantly to Judith Mitchell. Her lips moved, forming words of agreement.

"Yes, I'll leave as soon as possible."

Paul rolled onto his stomach to relieve the unnatural twist of his neck. His eyes narrowed at the sound of her voice, and the content of her words.

"Yes, I'll drive down and collect the boys on the way."

Judith's anxious voice rattled in Karen's ear. Enmeshed by a pair of eyes shading to black, Karen heard without hearing.

"I don't know." Impatience clawed at her nerves, her mind, her emotions. "Judith, I simply can't give you a definite time!" Karen could hear her own building anxiety and took a quick, settling breath. "I promise you, I will have the boys there as soon as possible.''

The panicky voice at the end of the line rattled again; Paul began to move. Karen's control snapped.

"I have a lot to do, Judith! And unless I get off this phone, I'll never get there! Yes. Goodbye.'' Without turning to look, Karen moved her arm to replace the receiver. Plastic clattered against plastic before the receiver nestled into the cradle. Paul was moving; Karen stopped breathing.

Paul came up off the floor with the liquid agility of a man half his age, his muscles tensed, as if ready to spring into whatever action proved necessary.

Karen's voice had been so low, so anxious, that he had heard only bits and pieces of her end of the conversation. But from her tone, Paul knew something was wrong, very wrong. Her face, moments before flushed with the soft glow of pleasurable satisfaction, was devoid of all color. Her eyes, recently slumbrous with repletion, were now wide and cloudy. Her mouth, seconds before full and moist from the caress of his lips, was now pinched and bracketed with lines of strain.

Her mouth.

The muscles lacing Paul's stomach clenched. Alarm billowed to encompass his tightening chest.

Karen's mouth was lost to him; he knew it. Despair invaded his mind and coiled deep down in his gut. He didn't go to her—he couldn't move, couldn't think. In that instant, not understanding why or how, Paul knew that when Karen's trembling white lips finally moved he would once again find himself outside in the cold, looking in, longing for warmth.

He wanted to curse. He wanted to scream a denial of the rejection not yet voiced. Paul stood motionless, unconscious of his nakedness, his narrowed gaze riveted to the stark expression on her face. Time froze for an endless instant. Encapsulated within that moment Paul felt the converging rush of anguished emotions and burgeoning, paralyzing fear. Supreme effort was required to form one word, a word that was like a death knell. "Karen?"

It was not unlike coming out of a trance. Karen blinked, and the timeless instant was over—everything was over. Pleasure and contentment were of a realm not intended for thirty-seven-year-old divorcées with teenage sons. Reality was shame, and self-disgust and pain. The pain she was feeling was streaking through her body now—the pain Charles had suffered while she had been taking her pleasure.

Karen shivered. The spell was broken. The harsh light of morning poured through the windows of the alcove, gilding Paul's tense body with spangles of gold. His nakedness was beautiful and so very natural, and yet it was an affront, an insult to her senses and shame.

"I must go." Her voice lacked substance; her eyes lacked life.

"Go? Go where?" Caution curled around the edges of his carefully controlled tone. "What has happened?"

"To New Hampshire to collect my boys, and then to Boston," she responded woodenly, her manner relaying unspoken words that pierced his heart with tiny poison darts. "Charles has had a heart attack, and he has been asking for me and his sons." Her throat worked, indicating more than the need to merely swallow. "I must go at once."

"Yes, of course you must go, but—"

Karen shook her head sharply, cutting off his words, cutting off his breath.

"There are no buts, Paul!" Her arms moved aimlessly. "I must leave at once!" As she moved, her bare sole made contact with a section of floor tile that had not been warmed by her flesh. A frown drew her eyebrows together as the sensation of chill enveloped her foot. Reluctantly, as if fearing what she'd see, Karen lowered her gaze.

Her glance skimmed, shied away, then came back to slowly examine her own unadorned body. She swayed from the strength of the shudder that tore through her. Memory flashed, too clear, too sharp, too damning. Vividly, as if rolled across a movie screen, a picture formed in her mind, a picture of two people, two *middle-aged* people, washed by sunlight, consumed by each other while in the throes of making love on the floor—no!—indulging their physical hungers!

The mental reenactment was demeaning, and it was demoralizing. What had seemed beautiful at the time took on shadings of ugliness. Karen swallowed against a rising tide of bitterness.

He had to stop her!

The silent inner command unlocked Paul's frozen muscles. Not even certain exactly what he had to stop Karen from doing or thinking, he knew he had to put a stop to it at once. Three long strides were all that were required to propel him from the dining alcove and across to where she stood, still hovering near the wall phone. Paul extended his hand as he took the third step. Karen flinched and shrank back.

Her act caused the second toll of the death knell sounding inside his head.

"Don't touch me, Paul, please." Karen knew she couldn't let him touch her. She couldn't bear to have him touch her—she'd collapse, fall apart, and she didn't have time to fall apart.

"Karen, what in hell is going on inside your head?" Paul's voice held more plea than demand.

"I'm naked!" Karen shouted. "You're naked!"

"So what?" he shouted back, frustration heavy in his voice. "What do clothes have to do with anything?"

Karen's head moved awkwardly as she glanced around, seeing nothing, feeling everything. "I've got to bathe and dress." Her breath lodged in her chest. "I've got to pack. *I've got to go for my boys!*"

Paul's hand flashed out to grasp her wrist as she spun away from him. "Hold it." His fingers tightened when she tried to yank free. "I said hold it, dammit!" His harsh tone stopped her frantic bid for release, but she refused to look at him. Paul's chest heaved with a soundless sigh. "That's better. I want you to tell me who you were speaking to on the phone and exactly what that person said to you to cause this hysterical reaction."

He wanted? *He* wanted? *Hysterical?* Anger ripped through Karen with the devastating force of a flash fire. She could look at him now; she could glare at him.

"Who do you think you are?" Karen's tone was scathing. God! She hurt, in her mind, in her heart and, worse, deep down in her soul—her so recently blackened soul. Her slicing tone cut into another soul, leaving it wounded and bleeding. "Just who in the hell do you think you are to question me?"

"Your lover."

Anger receded. Senses ceased rioting. Karen's brain switched to stun. It was an irrefutable fact: Paul Vanzant, wanderer, vagrant, whatever, was her lover. Conflict ascended. She was torn between two separate needs. Her arms ached to curl around his trim waist; her palm itched to slap his aristocratic face. She did neither. In a tone that was free of expression, Karen related the phone conversation to him—at least what she could remember of it. Paul's features settled into austere lines as she spoke.

"It's a flagrant imposition on ties that no longer bind." Breeding, culture and sheer male arrogance were expressed by Paul's tone.

"He's their father!" Karen protested, beginning to tremble. "Suppose it were you lying there in that hospital bed. Wouldn't you want your son, your daughter?"

Paul conceded the point with a slight inclination of his head. "Yes, of course. And I understand your willingness to take his sons to him." His lips flattened. "What I don't understand is your intense reaction to the news of his attack." He paused, as if hesitant to voice his suspicions. Then he squared his shoulders. "Are you still in love with him, Karen?"

"No." Simple truth rang in her voice. She shook her head. "No, Paul," she said more strongly, "I am not still in love with Charles. He very effectively killed the love I felt for him by confessing—or, more accurately, bragging—about his other women."

Paul's shoulders didn't slump with relief, though the urge was great. "All right. Then why all this panic?"

"My boys—" she began, her tone heating again.

"I understand that," he interrupted, slashing his hand through the air. "What I don't understand is your withdrawal." She opened her mouth; his hand slashed the air once more. "And you are, already have, withdrawn from me. I want to know why."

Why? Karen gaped at him. Didn't he know? Didn't he feel the slightest twinge of remorse? Couldn't he see exactly how that phone call had exposed their behavior? They were strangers—strangers! And yet, while her sons had gone innocently about their business and her sons' father had fought the pain of a heart attack, two strangers to one another had gone at each other like alley cats at mating time!

Didn't Paul see or understand that?

Karen's breath trembled from her quivering body on a sigh. No, of course Paul couldn't see or understand. He was a man, after all. And men viewed these things differently than women. Hadn't she had proof enough of exactly how men viewed the male-female relationship?

Her response was too long in coming. Paul's fingers tightened around her wrist.

"It was a mistake."

His fingers flexed, and Karen flinched.

"I'm sorry." The pressure was immediately eased. "What was a mistake?"

He knew. Karen was positive that though he had asked, Paul knew what her answer would be. She didn't hesitate.

"Us," she said, repressing a shudder. "The entire situation." Her gaze crept to the sunlit spot on the alcove carpet, then skittered away again. "Our, our—" She couldn't force the words past her lips.

"Our lovemaking, dammit!" Paul barked.

"It was all an enormous, dreadful mistake," Karen went on, as if his harsh definition had never reached her ears.

Paul's perfectly defined features grew taut with impatience. "Why?" he demanded harshly. "In what way was it a dreadful mistake?"

Though Karen trembled visibly, she met his drilling stare without flinching. "It all happened too soon. We don't know one another." Her trembling increased. "In simple terms, we were both motivated by lust, sex for sex's sake alone." Her trembling gave way to a violent shudder. "I—I feel as though I've not only betrayed myself but the trust of my children, as well," she said in a stark, shaken tone.

"And now you're drowning in guilt and shame and God knows what else." Paul's fingers loosened, releasing her imprisoned wrist. "You're wrong, you know." His voice held little hope of her hearing, or of her believing him if she did register his words.

Karen shook her head, confirming his lack of hope. She felt his sigh to the depths of her being—felt it, but could offer no solace to him, or to herself.

"I must go." Clutching the clothing to her now-chilled body, she turned away.

"Wait."

As had happened before, Karen found herself unable to disobey his commanding tone. She stopped but refused to look at him. "Paul, I must . . ."

"You must think about what you're doing," he finished for her. "You can't simply toss on some clothing, pack a bag and run out the door."

Since that was precisely what she'd been prepared to do, Karen glanced over her shoulder to frown at him. "Why can't I?"

"Has the house been secured?" he asked, oddly detached.

"No, but—"

"Do you have any idea of how long you'll be gone?"

"Well, no, but—"

"Have you notified the authorities at the boys' school to expect you?"

"You know I haven't!" Karen snapped, impatient with him and with herself. "But—"

"But what?" Paul's tone, his eyes, his attitude, were cool. He had accepted her decision; he had little choice at that emotional moment, but he couldn't accept hasty disorganization.

"I—" Karen's hands lifted, then fell. "I don't know."

"I do."

Her mind a whirling mass of feelings and confusion, Karen stared at him with dulled eyes. "Okay," she finally said. "If you know, tell me."

"I intend to." Paul swept a cool glance over her, then shifted his gaze to his own body. His lips twitched into a smile that was completely without humor. "The first thing we're going to do is dress. After that we're going to make fresh coffee, sit down and discuss what has to be done."

Karen launched into an argument. "But—"

"Karen," Paul snapped impatiently, "the only way to get started is to get started. Now please stop arguing and go get dressed."

Karen went, quickly, if not exactly at a dead run. By the time she was once more clothed and protected by the concealing garments of respectability, she felt more like herself. She was ready and able to cope with the situation—but she wouldn't allow herself to consider *which* situation.

As she rushed downstairs and into the kitchen, the realization hit her that Paul, on the other hand, was supremely ready to cope with any and all situations.

He was dressed in a knit pullover and faded jeans, jeans that should have looked odd on his elegant body but somehow looked perfect—perfectly fitting, perfectly appealing, perfectly sexy. And as if his attire wasn't demoralizing enough, he had cleared away their uneaten breakfast, loaded the dishwasher, brewed a fresh pot of coffee and warmed the blueberry muffins she'd planned to serve at lunchtime. Karen's renewed sense of confidence ebbed considerably.

"You didn't shower," she accused peevishly, trying to bolster her flagging ego.

"Of course I did." Paul spared her a chiding look as he carried the glass coffeepot to the table. "Sit down, have some coffee, and we'll plan the day." It wasn't an invitation, it was a direct order. "And bring the basket of muffins with you." He didn't bother glancing back to see if she'd comply; he obviously took it for granted that she would.

Karen bristled while she toyed with the idea of telling him precisely what he could do with the muffins, but on reflection decided it wasn't worth the effort. She had more important things to do than start a yelling match with a man she was unlikely to ever see again after they left the house and parted company.

Unlikely to ever see again. The echoing phrase induced a weakness that conflicted with the nervous energy urging her into constructive action. Wanting to run, possibly in several different directions at once, Karen snatched up the basket and followed him to the table.

Silence prevailed for long moments; tearing silence, brittle silence, an "I'll scream if it doesn't end" silence. Yet, when Paul quietly broke the silence, Karen started as though he'd shouted.

"You are taking the car?"

"What?" she asked blankly.

Paul regarded her with infinite patience. "The car, Karen. I assume the compact I saw in the garage earlier is yours."

"Oh! Yes. It is mine, and I am taking it."

"Where in New Hampshire is this prep school?"

The school. Her boys. Karen fought back a resurgence of shame and guilt.

"Karen?" His patience was not quite as infinite.

"Ah . . . halfway," she replied vaguely.

"Hmm." Paul murmured into his cup before very casually placing it on the matching saucer. "Halfway from where to where?'' His lowering tone and brow finally got through to her.

''I'm sorry!'' She flushed. ''The school is approximately midway between here and Boston.'' Her shoulders tilted in a helpless shrug. ''The location of the school was a symbolic concession under the terms of the divorce.'' Her smile didn't quite make it. ''An indication that, symbolically at least, Charles and I are still sharing the children.''

''I wouldn't touch that statement with a forked stick,'' Paul commented, knowing full well his derisive tone said it all.

''I know.'' Karen sighed her weariness. ''Could we get on with the plans, please?'' Arching her brows, she reached for a muffin she really didn't want.

Paul continued. Succinctly, concisely, he outlined exactly what he considered had to be done; naturally, he was absolutely right on every point. While he spoke, Karen nodded, agreeing with every suggestion, and crumbled the muffin onto her plate.

''Fodder for the gulls?''

Karen trailed his gaze to the tiny pile of crumbs on her plate. ''I'm not hungry,'' she said defensively.

Paul's lips curved into a small smile lightly tinged with tenderness. ''A dead giveaway to your emotional condition,'' he observed, referring to her earlier admission regarding her love of food.

''I suppose.'' Karen tossed the agreement out carelessly, making it clear she was not about to allow him to reopen that particular topic. Paul got the message.

''You have friends in Boston?'' he asked with a fine display of restraint. ''People you can spend time with while you're there?''

"Oh, yes." She offered him her first genuine smile since answering the phone. "I also have my business there."

"Business?" Paul sat up straight. "What sort of business?"

"I own a specialty shop... fine gifts, china, bric-a-brac and such. It's called Garnishes." She grimaced. "Of course, being way up here in Maine, I no longer manage it myself. Charles has been overseeing it for me." At the thought and mention of her former husband's name, Karen wet her suddenly dry lips. "I'll need to make other arrangements."

"A modern, civilized divorce," he muttered, harking back to the confidences she'd made in a wine-induced haze. "And yet another statement I wouldn't touch with—"

"All right!" Karen snapped, pushing her chair away from the table. "Shouldn't we get on with what must be done?" As she was already crossing the kitchen floor to the sink, he had little choice.

The full October harvest moon blessed the landscape with shimmering silvery light and danced in a glittering path on the cresting sea.

Huddled inside her robe, cold even in the warmth of her bedroom, Karen stood at the window, staring into the brightness of the night and the darkness of her thoughts.

A few feet behind her, her small bedside clock rhythmically ticked away the minutes of the night. The alarm on the clock was set for six. All was in readiness. Due entirely to Paul's penchant for detail, the house was secure, made safe in the event Karen's stay in Boston should turn out to be an extended one. Except for the windows she stared out of and the two in Paul's room across the hall, all the windows in the house were covered by sturdy, locked shutters. The solid wood storm doors were in place at the front and back of the house. Her nearest neighbor had been contacted and informed that Karen would be away; the taciturn neighbor had said he'd check on the property every day. A large suitcase and a garment bag had been packed and were now in the corner by the door. She had talked to her sons' guidance counselor; he had assured her he would break the news about their father gently to the boys and have them ready to leave when she arrived at the school. Her car had been checked out and the gas tank filled at the service station in the small town. Karen planned to leave the house by 6:30.

Every contingency that could have been thought of had been thought of by Paul. The single thing left for Karen to do was to get some much-needed sleep, but for her, sleep was elusive. At 10:20 on a sparkling autumn night, Karen was wakeful with thoughts of her lover.

What was he doing now, this very moment, as she stared into a sea reflecting the restlessness she was feeling. Was he asleep? Karen's chest heaved in a deep sigh. Confused, torn by emotional conflict, she had deliberately distanced herself from him. Throughout that long, busy day, while tension had crackled between them, the atmosphere had been cool.

But the distancing was of her own choosing; the coolness was what she preferred, wasn't it? Despair sank like a weight in her stomach. Denying the sensation, Karen squared her shoulders and raised her chin. Yes, of course she preferred the cool distance. She'd had her moment of self-indulgence; it was now time to pay the price.

The cost was high, in terms of self-esteem, in terms of mental anguish, in terms of self-respect. Karen bit her lip as her mind cried a protest.

She was not a loose woman easily used!

A soft, choking sob challenged the silence of the night. She wanted the distance between them, yes. But couldn't he have fought against her decision, just a little? Had Paul had to accept it without the least resistance?

The previous night's storm had moved out to sea, leaving behind tranquillity. Outside, the night was calm. Inside Paul, a storm raged fiercely, creating havoc and disruption.

He wanted to be fair. He was trying to be understanding. But he was fighting a losing battle within himself, because most of all he simply wanted. Denying that want, Paul paced the large, comfortable room, fingers raking through his silver-kissed dark hair at regular intervals.

He hurt in all the ways there were to hurt—in body, mind and emotions. And although he readily admitted that he had absolutely no right to interfere with Karen's decisions, admitting that didn't make the hurt easier to bear.

Paul's narrowed gaze sliced to the closed bedroom door; his mind's eye sliced through it and the door directly across the wide hallway. Was Karen sleeping? His inner vision created images of her that drew a muffled curse from him.

Of all the inopportune times for that bastard to— Paul cut the thought short, surprised by its vehemence. Even in his burning hell of wanting, Paul could not accuse Charles Mitchell of deliberately suffering a heart attack simply to interfere with his ex-wife's love affair.

Halting at the window, Paul stared bleakly into the night. Besides, he reasoned, exhaling a sigh, even without the call about her former husband, Karen probably would have discovered another reason to withdraw from him, even if she'd had to manufacture one. The call might have precipitated the withdrawal, but he felt positive that it would have come anyway before too long. Paul was even positive he knew why she would have withdrawn.

To a man of Paul's intelligence and experience, reading Karen's character was not at all difficult. Although certainly not without its complexities, Karen's personality was as clear as the cloudless fall sky spread out before him. She was genuinely a good, moral person. She very obviously believed in right and wrong and lived her life accordingly. She worked hard and stood firm on matters of principle, and since that damned call, her principles were giving her hell about sleeping with a man she barely knew. Paul accepted her decision—at least he was trying to.

Heaven knew it wasn't easy. But the fact that he'd found Karen after years of believing he'd lost the ability to cherish a woman like her made acceptance more difficult. What they had shared, the sheer beauty of that sharing, had left a mark, a greedy hunger in every cell in Paul's body. And he believed Karen was special—how else could he explain her seemingly effortless power to arouse him, to awaken the sensuality in him? Oh, yes, Karen was definitely special to him. She was the kind of woman a man wanted by his side—in good times, in bad times, in his home, in his bed.

Merely thinking the word "bed" tightened every muscle in Paul's body. *Karen.* He needed her. But therein lay the cause of his dilemma. Because he had needed her too soon and had given in to that need too soon, he had shaken her, forced her to question herself as a person. He was now paying for his hasty actions and, he felt sure, would continue to pay.

The piper has presented his bill.

Paul grimaced as the thought crept into his mind. Instinctively he knew he would be facing a long, cold winter. He also knew that he would survive; he had already survived more than six years of endless winter. This autumn had been a reprieve, a tantalizing breath of spring, a zephyr of renewal on the barren plain of his frozen soul.

Eyes shut, Paul endured a violent shiver. He didn't want to go back to being dead in spirit. He had been captivated by the heady waltz of life. Opening his eyes, he turned to look at the closed bedroom door.

The piper has presented his bill.

As he took his first stride toward the door, a grim smile tilted the corners of Paul's lips. He would pay the bill without complaint. But nothing—not heaven, not hell and not Karen Mitchell—would stop him that night. Paul's jaw firmed as he pulled the door open.

He would pay the bill—but he would have one last dance.

Chapter Six

Paul didn't knock. Grasping the doorknob, he turned it and pushed the door open. He didn't wait for an invitation to enter the room, either. His expression determined, he walked into the room.

"Paul?" Karen's startled whisper was nearly drowned by the sound of the door banging against the wall. Her body stiffened visibly; her eyes widened with apprehension and, Paul thought, hopefully, a tiny spark of suppressed excitement. "What—what do you want?"

Talk about obvious questions! Paul might have laughed, and he was tempted to smile, but he couldn't manage either expression. Hell, he realized with a jolt of shock, he could barely breathe!

The slant to his raised eyebrow was rakish; the slant on his lips was pure enticement. Paul had no way of knowing the toe-curling effect his appearance had on his quarry. Moving slowly, he crossed the room to where she stood, framed by the window at her back.

He was barefoot, and the pads of his feet made soundless contact with the soft carpet. *Stalking!* The word flashed into his mind and shivered the length of his spine. He suddenly felt slightly light-headed, and his pace nearly faltered. *Stalking.* It was a heady thought, conjuring up images of strong, silent predators closing in on the desired prey.

Paul savored the feeling, liking it, relishing the vision of himself as the hunter—he, Vanzant, the man who was more king of the carpeted boardroom than of the broad savannas. He tingled with all kinds of anticipatory thrills.

"Paul?"

Her voice was hoarse, reedy with emotion. Paul absorbed the sound of it into his expanding fantasy. She was his, if not forever, at least for this last night. All he had to do was stalk...and take. The realization dissolved the last lingering thread of hesitation and doubt. He had spent his life giving. He had surrendered his manhood giving. For this one night, he was finished with giving. He would take anything, everything he wanted. His stride firm, Paul advanced on the woman he could taste with every one of his clamoring senses.

She knew what to expect. With heightened tension, Paul could see understanding flare deep in her eyes. Flecks of gold excitement sparked within the brown depths. She was fighting a battle with self-denial. Paul could actually see the inner war being waged. The visible proof of her struggle against herself increased his own tension to an unbearable heat. And he could see the instant need for surrender weakened her resistance.

As he came to a stop inches from her, Paul threw back his head and laughed; the sound was not unlike the victory roar of the deadly jungle beast.

Karen was his!

His laughter thrilled and frightened her at one and the same time. There was something different about Paul this night; he was not the same man who had drawn her with such care and tenderness onto the floor of the dining alcove that morning. The man she now faced revealed not a trace of tenderness. Sheer male animal gleamed from his narrowed dark eyes, a feral male animal on the scent of his mate. His appearance terrified her with excitement.

Wanting him, and afraid of the intensity of her own sudden wild, inexplicable needs, Karen stopped breathing and slid one foot back, edging away from him. The smile that curved his lips halted her shifting foot. Karen froze for an instant that was an eternity. Then, gasping, she spun away.

Her movement came too late. Paul's arm whipped out, and his fingers wrapped around her wrist. With the most negligent of tugs, he whirled her around. Her chest collided with his, igniting fires in places in her body that were already warm and willing. Before she could draw a full breath, he was swinging her up into his arms. With three long strides, Paul was by the side of the bed. He grunted, and the sound was one of deep pleasure. Then he lifted her up, high, and tossed her onto the bed.

"Paul!" The cry exploded from Karen, a one-word protest that lacked conviction. "What do you think you're doing?"

Paul paused in the sublimely casual act of removing his robe to glide a calculating glance at the enticing length of her body. She was clad in a sheer nightgown. One dark eyebrow peaked tauntingly.

"I'm going to give you a memory to take with you to Boston."

Tension coiled over her shoulders to converge in a knot at the back of her neck. Applying conscious effort, Karen eased the white-knuckled grip she had on the steering wheel. The road undulated in front of her like an unwinding ribbon, moving her toward a reunion with her sons and uncertainty about their father. Behind her, the road of ribbon whipped back, and contained a long expensive car.

Karen flicked a glance into the rearview mirror and felt the knot in her neck contract. The midnight-blue vehicle gleaming in the pure sunlight of a perfect Indian-summer day trailed her small compact at a safe distance of three hundred feet. But before too long, the road behind her would be empty, regardless of how many vehicles replaced it on the highway. The first leg of her journey lay a little more than an hour away; Paul would be going in another direction after they parted company near the town where the small, exclusive prep school was located.

The edges of the road blurred as a film of tears misted her eyes. Lifting one hand from the wheel, she brushed her fingertips impatiently over her eyelids. The midnight-blue car shot past her as her vision cleared. Startled, Karen sniffed and frowned as the right rear turn signal on the blue car began to pulse. Without conscious thought, she followed the larger vehicle off the road and into the parking lot of a small, rustic-looking restaurant.

Paul stepped out of his car as she parked alongside his vehicle. "Time for a break," he said, opening her door for her.

Gathering the remnants of her emotional control, Karen nodded and suppressed a sigh. It was not time for a break; it was time for them to go their separate ways. They were within an hour of the school and her boys. And, she realized, taking note of their location, they were minutes from the interstate exchange. Paul would change direction at the interstate. She would go on to—Karen blinked rapidly, fighting a fresh surge of tears.

She had spent the morning deliberately not thinking of the night before, and she couldn't afford to think about it now. Raising her chin, Karen stared off into the distance and felt a sharp pang in the center of her chest. Farther north, in Maine, the terrain lay barren and ready for winter. But here, a little farther south in New Hampshire, autumn clung to the landscape with a fading glory. Even muted, the colors were beautiful and an affront to her senses. Karen wasn't aware that she had come to a stop to stare resentfully at nature's display until Paul voiced a quiet observation.

"The blaze must have been fantastic a short time ago."

His low-pitched voice jolted through her, leaving a hollow sensation in the pit of her being. He was referring to the colors of the panoramic landscape, but Karen applied his comment to the scene they had acted out the night before. And the blaze had indeed been fantastic. Glancing up at him, she suddenly felt as empty and barren as the Maine coast.

"I'm hungry." Her voice was rough, but Karen didn't care. She hurt. Dragging her gaze from his somber face and avoiding the insult of the surrounding color, she rammed her hands into the side pockets of her soft wool slacks and strode toward the entrance of the restaurant. She told herself that she didn't care whether or not Paul followed her. She almost believed it, but then she was becoming adept at lying to herself.

"Karen?"

Paul was at her heels—like a well-trained pet, Karen thought, fighting the insidious spread of pain. But she knew this man was no pet, no sleek, well-schooled tabby. Not Paul. No, hidden behind this man's facade of elegance and sophistication a tiger crouched, ready to spring and devour when aroused. Karen's soul bore the scars of his teeth and claws.

Her silent analogy induced a shiver deep inside her that threatened to release scrupulously buried memories. Terrified she'd drown should the flow escape, Karen yanked open the door and entered the restaurant. The smile she offered the hostess was much too bright and hurt like fury.

"Two?" The hostess was middle-aged and had a pleasant face; her smile was practiced yet attractive.

"Yes, please."

"At a window," Paul inserted in an authoritative tone. "We want to enjoy what's left of the foliage."

The smile he offered the hostess transformed the older woman's from plastic to the genuine article.

Watching the woman bloom beneath the warmth of Paul's exceptional good looks and charm, Karen experienced a thrill of vindication; she *wasn't* the only woman to feel an immediate attraction to him. Small consolation perhaps, but when one was desperate, one clung to even tiny shreds of pride.

The table was placed directly before a wide, undraped window that afforded a spectacular view of the gently rolling countryside. Red, orange, rust and splashes of green dazzled the eyes of any and all beholders. Karen lowered her gaze to the linen-covered tabletop.

"We must talk."

Karen's fingers clenched on the small luncheon menu the hostess had placed in front of her. Paul had said exactly the same words to her that morning as they'd stood drinking a cup of coffee at the kitchen counter. He had repeated the words as they'd stood at the rear of her car after loading her luggage into the small trunk. Now, as she had earlier, Karen shook her head.

"There's nothing to talk about." Absently moving her left hand, she stroked one finger the length of the tines of her fork. "You're going home. I'm going to Boston. End of story."

"No, dammit! That's not the—Karen!" His tone, which had been sharp with annoyance, softened with concern at her involuntary gasp. Karen had pierced the tip of her finger with the tine.

Karen dismissed his concern with a shrug as she stared dispassionately at a tiny drop of blood. "It's nothing.'' Her right hand was groping for a napkin when Paul grasped her left hand and drew the injured finger to his lips. The touch of his lips against her skin was excruciating; the flick of his tongue against the tiny puncture was devastating and threatened to undo Karen's precious store of composure.

"Paul, please don't," she protested in a strangled tone, tugging her hand back. His hold on her tightened.

"God, Karen, don't look at me like that." His breath misted her flesh, and the agonized sound of his voice misted her thoughts.

"Like—like what?" Karen could barely speak for the thickness in her throat.

"Like . . ." Paul lowered his eyes as he turned her hand, exposing her palm to his lips. "Like you've been dealt a killing blow." He reverently touched his mouth to her palm.

Karen felt his kiss like a stiletto thrust to her heart. She tugged reflexively against his grip. Paul began to raise his eyes at her action. His eyes flickered and widened as his gaze noted a crescent-shaped bruise on the inside of her wrist. His curse was all the more shocking for the very softness of it.

"I've marked you." His gaze seared the bruise. "And I've hurt you—" his breath shuddered from his body "—in so many ways." His lips bestowed a quivering blessing on the mark. "I'm sorry, Karen. I never meant to hurt you in any way."

"I know." Karen had to pause to swallow, to breathe, to absorb the tremors racing up her arm from her wrist.

While she hesitated, Paul glanced up. His night-black eyes betrayed regret, resignation. "I don't want to leave you here like this." His grip on her wrist tightened as a shiver moved through her body. "Karen, let me follow you into Boston." His voice was rough with strain.

"No!" Karen shook her head and pulled her hand from his grasp. A vision rose to torment her mind, an image of herself attempting to explain Paul's presence to her sons. Mark, her baby, was still young enough at thirteen to accept as fact whatever his mother told him. But her eldest had developed into a very savvy fifteen-year-old. Rand would immediately identify and disdain the relationship between his mother and a man other than his father. "No," she repeated, drowning in a fresh flood of guilt and shame. "It's impossible."

"It's not impossible. Nothing—" He stopped speaking as a young waitress approached the table to take their order. Paul cursed under his breath and snatched up the menu.

Karen lowered her gaze to the cardboard that was quivering suspiciously in her hand. But her reprieve was short-lived. Paul resumed the argument the instant the waitress moved on to another table. Karen had already forgotten what she'd ordered.

"Karen, I can wait in a hotel. You can't be expected to spend every waking hour with your sons or cooling your heels in a hospital." Lines of tension scored his face, revealing his frustration and, for the first time since she'd met him, his age.

"No, Paul." Karen rushed the refusal, too tempted to give in to his suggestion. "I'd have to explain..."

The expression in the eyes she raised to his was stark, reflecting her inner conflict. She took a breath before continuing. "I'd have to explain to my boys, Charles, his parents. How could I make them understand something I don't understand myself, about myself?"

"You're a mature woman, Karen!" Paul exclaimed softly. "Except for the possibility of your children, you don't owe explanations to anyone." His voice lowered dangerously. "Least of all to that—"

"Paul!" Karen's shocked voice cut across his low snarl. She glanced around quickly to see if he'd been overheard. Their nearest neighbors, a middle-aged foursome, were busily discussing the merits of the menu, quite oblivious to the drama close at hand. "Name-calling solves nothing! Don't you understand? I *can't* continue. It's impossible."

Paul's eyes gleamed with a mounting anger that masked a sense of desperation. "And I'm telling you nothing's impossible, not if you want it badly enough." His tone hardened. "And I want it badly, Karen. You'll probably never know how very badly I want it."

Want. The single word hammered inside Karen's mind while the waitress served the meal. *Want.* The echo of it mocked her throughout the ordeal of making believe she was eating the sandwich she couldn't remember ordering and didn't taste even as she consumed it. *Want.* Dammit! It was the wanting that had placed her in this untenable hell of guilt in the first place.

He had wanted. She had wanted. And because they had appeased their wants with one another, she was now suffering the pain of self-doubt and shame.

"Karen, we need to talk," Paul said urgently as she placed her empty coffee cup on its delicate saucer. "Let me follow you. Meet with me in Boston. I'll give you my word that I won't touch you. I'll give you all the time you need to sort out your feelings. But let's at least talk it out. I want to explain..."

Karen had had it with the word "want." Pushing her chair back, she surged to her feet and hurried from the restaurant. She wanted nothing more at that moment than to never hear the word *want* again for as long as she lived.

Paul caught up to her as she was fumbling to unlock her car. He didn't try to restrain her. At least, not physically. The soft urgency of his tone was restraint in itself.

"You're going to throw it away, aren't you?"

At the end of her patience, pulled off balance by conflicting needs and emotions, Karen turned on him, lashing out.

"Throw all *what* away?" she demanded, angry and scared. "We don't know each other. We don't even know if we like one another! We felt an attraction, a highly combustible chemical attraction, and we both responded to it." Her shoulders drooped. "But now it's time for reality." Karen forced herself to look at him. "You have a family, a life in Philadelphia. And I have two boys who may be facing the possibility of losing their father. I think someone once said that when reality walks in the door, sensuality flies out the window. The window is open, Paul. The time for flight is now."

"It's not true." Paul smiled faintly as she began to frown. "I do know that I like you. You are very easy to like."

For one fleeting instant, Karen's smile rivaled the brilliance of the sun-sparkled day. Then it was gone, as was the light of hope that had sprung to life in Paul's eyes. Obeying an impulse, she reached out to touch him. Then, just as quickly, she withdrew her hand.

"I like you, too." Her smile had the power to break a cynic's heart. "You're bossy as hell, but I like you, Paul Vanzant."

"Karen." He moved toward her, but she was faster, opening the door and slipping behind the wheel.

"I must go," she said, her voice edged with desperation. "They're expecting me." She bit her lip, then looked up at him. "I'll never forget you. Goodbye, Paul." She pulled the door closed between them.

"Karen!"

The sound of the engine roaring to life muffled his cry of protest. Throwing the car into reverse, she backed the vehicle away from him. Again she hesitated, staring at him as if unable to tear her eyes away. Then she spun the wheel. Tires screeched, and the car shot forward. Karen heard Paul's angry voice through the closed window.

"Damn you, Karen!"

"Will Dad be all right, Mom?"

Stifling a sigh, Karen managed a patient smile instead. It was at least the dozenth time her youngest son had asked that same question.

"I don't know, honey," Karen answered honestly. "Grandma didn't know when I spoke to her. It was too soon after the attack. But hopefully by the time we reach Boston the doctors will have more information for us."

"I don't want Dad to die, Mom." Fear reduced Mark's voice to that of a very young child's.

"Oh, honey." Karen reached across the seat to grasp the boy's hand. "I know. I know." Understanding and compassion clenched at her chest. "Try not to think about it." Karen hated being reduced to trite, inane motherly platitudes, but as a mother, what option did she have? "Just hope, and pray, and—"

"Dad's not going to die, ya nerd." The jeer of disgust came from the half boy, half man sprawled on the back seat.

"Rand," Karen murmured warningly, capturing his reflection in the rearview mirror.

"Well, does he hafta whine and talk so dumb?" Rand argued defensively.

"But I'm scared!" Mark sniffled. "What will we do if he—"

"Will ya stuff it?" Rand's voice rose, then cracked.

"Randolf!"

"Aw, Mom!" The boy glared into the mirror at her for a moment, then quickly lowered his gaze. Rand was not quick enough to hide the sheen of tears in his eyes.

Karen's fingers contracted around the abused steering wheel. Rand was every bit as frightened as

Mark was; his belligerence was a ruse to conceal his fear and uncertainty. Karen longed to comfort both boys, reassure them, soothe them as she had when they had been small and had run to her with scrapes and bruises. If only she could hug them and kiss them and make it better, she thought, feeling suddenly inadequate and unequal to the task before her.

Without conscious direction, Karen's gaze sought the mirror, not to seek the wounded eyes of her son but to study the highway unwinding behind her. There were all types of vehicles jockeying for position on the multilane highway, but not one of them was painted a midnight blue.

A man is never there when you really need him, she told herself, her throat working to ease a growing tightness.

With her youngest son weeping softly on the seat beside her and her eldest alternately yelling at him, then pleading with him to "bag it," Karen was much too upset and distracted to consider the incongruity of her blanket condemnation of men, most particularly the man she had refused to have there when she needed him. She was hurting on more levels than she'd ever realized there were. She was tired. She felt alone, really alone, for the first time in her adult life. She felt too close to the edge of defeat. She was beginning to get frightened, and beginning to question her ability to cope with the traumatic effect on her sons in the event Charles succumbed to the heart attack.

He can't die! The protest rang inside her head, accompanied by one boy's sobs and another boy's muttered imprecations. Damn you, Charles Mitchell, don't you dare die!

Karen's glance flicked to the mirror.

Oh, God, Paul, where are you?

Where was she now? Nearing Boston? In Boston? Perhaps already at the hospital—with Charles?

Paul grunted in self-disgust and sliced a resentful glance at his wristwatch. He had promised himself he would not think about her. He had warned himself he could not afford to think about her. He had failed miserably to keep his promise.

How had her sons reacted to the news about their father? Paul sighed. Karen's boys were another subject he had vowed not to consider. But dammit! he said to himself, he was a parent, too! He had raised a son through the difficult teenage years. He knew firsthand how very deeply children felt about all kinds of things, important and mundane. They would be a handful for her, Paul decided, his tight lips smoothing into a gentle smile of reminiscence. Hell, children were usually a handful, even on the best of days!

She should have support.

The tightness was back, flattening his lips. He should be with her. He had wanted to be with her. He still wanted to be there for her.

Where *was* she now?

With favorable driving conditions, Karen could be in the city and at the hospital by now. Was the bas— Paul cut his thought short. Had Charles Mitchell's condition improved at all? Paul sincerely hoped so. He hoped so for the boys' sake. He hoped so for Karen's sake. And, not even sure why, he hoped so for his own sake.

He missed her. It had been only a matter of hours since she'd left him breathing in the exhaust fumes from her car as she'd roared out of the parking lot, and yet he missed her like hell on fire. Paul exhaled heavily. With his control on his mental responses undermined, memories of the previous night rushed to the fore to tease his senses and torment his body.

Lord! Had he really behaved like that, all macho and masterful? The mere concept boggled his mind. Never, never before in his life, had Paul displayed such aroused heat or such vigor! And damn him if he hadn't reveled in every second of the display.

Paul's thigh muscles grew taut; he shifted on the leather seat. How, he wondered, was Karen feeling about her own responses and participation in the previous night's activities? She'd refused to discuss it that morning, had in fact shied away from even looking directly at him until they had stopped for lunch. Paul grimaced. Had he succeeded in adding more self-doubt and guilt to her overscrupulous conscience? He fervently hoped not, yet feared he had.

Paul's spirit flagged. He had an empty feeling that warned him he'd be missing Karen Mitchell for a long time to come.

Karen greeted the usual tangle of midafternoon traffic in Boston with a heartfelt sigh of relief. Her spirit felt battered from having to constantly comfort her sons.

She had a pounding headache from the increasing pressure of the tension at the back of her neck. Her eyes were gritty from incipient tears and the lack of sleep the night before. And her mind felt abused from fighting the memories of why she hadn't slept the night before. In comparison, the need to maneuver the crazy-quilt mess of one-way traffic in the historic city was a piece of cake.

"Are we going to Grandma's first?" Mark asked.

Karen stole a glance from the street to offer her son a smile. "No, honey. I think both Grandma and Grandpa will be at the hospital."

"Are we soon there?"

Karen frowned at his grammar. "Just a little while longer, honey," she replied, striving to hang on to her control.

"I'm hungry," he whimpered.

"You're always hungry," his brother taunted from the back.

"As a matter of fact, I'm hungry, too," Karen said brightly, giving her oldest a quelling look via the rear-view mirror. "We can get something to eat in the hospital coffee shop as soon as we find out how your dad's doing. Okay?"

"Okay," Mark agreed.

"Now take a break," came the hard-voiced order from the back seat.

Karen's eyes shot to the mirror to catch his reflection with a "this is your mother speaking and I'm not kidding" look. Rand lowered his eyes.

For a few moments, relative peace and quiet prevailed—at least inside the car. Outside it was a different story. A motorist running a yellow light missed her car by a breath. As she attempted to push the brake pedal through the floor of the car with her foot, Karen flung her right arm out in front of Mark to back up his seat belt.

Mark decided that was the perfect time to begin wailing. "I hate this! I hate this whole day!" he sobbed. "We're all gonna die."

"Mark, please!" Karen eased the car back into the flow of traffic and her temper back into submission. "It was close," she said soothingly, silently cursing the ancestry of the other driver. "But we're fine, and no one is going to die." Brave words, she jeered at herself.

"Boy, are you really thirteen?" Rand asked sarcastically.

Karen prayed for enlightened motorists and spared another warning glare for her back-seat agitator.

Mark then made the mistake of wriggling in his seat. "I have to go to the bathroom."

"You always hafta go to the bathroom. All you ever do is eat and go to the bathroom," Rand gibed.

Karen's patience gave up the battle. "Rand, I've had enough of your snide remarks. What in the world is the matter with you?" Her eyes shifted back and forth between the street and the mirror; she saw her firstborn drop his head abjectly. Her heart clenched as she heard his whispered cry.

"Oh, Mom. I'm so scared."

Chapter Seven

Karen ached to bring the car to a dead stop right there in the middle of the nightmarish traffic and bawl with her two offspring, both of whom were sobbing now. Gritting her teeth and murmuring garbled words of comfort, she wove the car in and around the vehicular maze leading to the hospital.

After finally securing a place to park, she rushed the boys into the hospital, past the information desk and straight into the first visitors' lounge she came to. Breathing a sigh of relief at finding the room empty, Karen dropped her purse onto the nearest chair and swept Rand and Mark into her arms.

"Okay, now cry it out," she coaxed softly. "It'll help."

Neither of the boys held back. The dam of fear and anxiety burst, and Karen tightened her arms, absorbing her sons' shudders into her body. The moment was bittersweet for Karen. It had been some time since either of the boys had sought succor in her embrace, and an especially long time for Rand. At odd moments, catching herself gazing wistfully at an infant or toddler and consumed with a longing to cradle the child to her breast, she wondered if she was suffering the empty-nest syndrome. Usually the sensation of emptiness was fleeting and she went back to the reality of the present convinced that she was content with her life. Now, fiercely clasping their slim bodies to her heart, Karen wondered again.

Ignoring the tears stinging her eyes, she closed them and brushed one damp cheek over Rand's tangled hair and the other over Mark's tousled curls.

For this tiny, isolated moment, the boys were hers again, her beautiful babies. Soon, too soon, they would collect themselves, she knew. Very likely, Rand would be first. Then, together, they would go face the news about their father. But until then, Karen would savor the sweet feeling of being needed by her babies, even if the feeling was transient and contained equal amounts of pleasure and pain. As she had suspected, Rand was the first to withdraw.

"I forgot a hankie," he mumbled, avoiding her eyes by swiping at his nose with the back of his hand.

"There are tissues in my purse." She indicated the bag with a movement of her hand. "Give some to your brother, please." She was unable to keep her hand from creeping to the back of Mark's head, and her fingers stroked his fine curly hair. With a final snorting gulp, Mark stepped back.

"I didn't wanna act like a baby." Mark shot a fearful look at his brother, the infamous tormentor.

"Who did?" Rand muttered, absolving Mark of guilt, while shoving a wad of tissues into his hand.

"Neither one of you have..." Karen began.

"Only little kids cry," Mark sniffled.

"Sez who?" Rand demanded, mopping the moisture from his lean cheeks.

"Dad," Mark said, following his idol's example and applying damp tissue to his even damper face. "He said real men never cry."

Sounds exactly like something your dad would say, Karen thought, shaking her head. "Men are human, Mark, and all humans experience a need to relieve fear and pain at times," she said softly.

"Dad don't ever cry," Mark insisted.

"No," Rand agreed in a surprisingly adult tone. "Dad swears."

"Yeah, he does!" Mark blinked, startled. "He swears a lot!"

"Yeah." Rand's tone aged with a hint of cynicism. "Dad swears an awful lot."

In Karen's opinion, Charles's penchant for the more colorful expletives left a lot to be desired. She also thought that this particular vein of conversation had run out. "Well, given a choice," she observed, "I prefer tears to cursing as an outlet for easing stress." She ran an appraising glance over their faces as she picked up her purse. "You guys ready?"

Mark's face pinched. Karen noted the boy's frozen expression at the same instant Rand did. Rand moved faster. Stepping to his brother, Rand slung a thin arm around Mark's drooping shoulders.

"C'mon, punk," he said roughly. "Whaddaya wanna bet Dad's gonna be all right?"

"D'ya think?" The hopeful, trusting look on Mark's face was enough to break a mother's heart.

Somehow, from some hidden wellspring of maturing strength, Rand found a grin. "Sure," he said with a confidence Karen was certain he didn't feel. "I'd put my allowance on it."

Strong words indeed. Karen smiled mistily, her chest expanding with pride for her boy, who was almost a man. Fighting back a resurgence of tears, she walked briskly to the door. "Come on, Mark," she said, extending her hand to him. "We'd better go, before your brother discovers he's wagered all of his junk-food money and goes into pizza withdrawal."

They found Judith Mitchell pacing the visitors' lounge outside the closed doors of the coronary unit. Tears flooded the slender, attractive woman's eyes at the sight of her grandsons.

"Oh, my poor darlings!" Judith rushed to embrace the boys.

Alarm flared inside Karen as Judith enfolded the boys protectively in her arms. "Is Charles worse?" she asked in a voice hoarse with strain.

"Worse?" Judith glanced up and blinked. "Oh! Oh, no." She shook her head distractedly and tightened her hold on the now-squirming boys. "In fact, he's much improved."

The boys made good their escape; Karen's relieved breath escaped. Suddenly she wanted to hug Judith— dear, sweet, *vague* Judith. Giving in to the urge, she stepped into the older woman's deserted arms.

"I'm so glad," she murmured, hugging the woman tightly before stepping back. "Tell us everything, please."

Judith's hand fluttered, the absent, helpless motion a clear reflection of the woman herself. Karen had always loved her former mother-in-law; it was impossible not to love the endearing woman. But Judith was just a trifle airy.

"Well, I don't know too much myself," Judith began, fortunately not noticing Rand's "tell us about it" expression.

Karen was back to shooting quelling glances at her not-yet-a-man son. "Then tell us what you do know," she said, gently prompting the frowning woman.

"When we arrived this morning," Judith replied at once, "the nurse told us simply that Charles was much improved." She glanced wistfully at the coronary unit's closed doors. "The specialist is in with Charles now, and so is Randolf." Her gaze drifted back to Karen. "They've been in there a long time, since right after lunchtime."

"I see." Karen gnawed on her lower lip, trying to decide whether the lengthy consultation boded good or bad. The fact that Charles's father, Randolf J. Mitchell, had been allowed to be present during the doctor's visit was unsurprising; Randolf was a member of the hospital's board of directors. She was beginning to get fidgety when she noticed Mark squirming in the chair he'd dropped into. Karen expelled a sigh and looked at Judith.

"Are there public rest rooms nearby?" A maternal smile curved her lips. "Your youngest grandson is in dire need."

"Of course!" Judith literally leaped at the excuse to be doing something. "Come along, darling." She held her hand out to Mark as if to a toddler. "I'll take you."

For a flickering instant, sheer horror was reflected in the boy's eyes. Rand hid a burst of laughter behind a cough. Then, realizing his grandmother wouldn't dream of actually going into the room with him, Mark sprang from the chair. As the two exited the room, Karen heard her baby go to work on his doting grandparent.

"Is there someplace we could get something to eat in here?" Mark was heard to ask plaintively. "We didn't stop all the way down here, and I'm hungry, Grandma."

Though her reply was unintelligible, Judith's tone conveyed anxious concern for her darling. Karen smiled, and Rand shook his head.

"What a little con artist," he said, grinning his respect for his brother's talent. "Boy, he can always hook Grandma with one soulful look from his big brown eyes." His grin faded, and he was quiet for a moment. "I guess," he finally continued, a smile that was too wise and too full of acceptance curving his lips, "it's because he looks so much like Dad."

Karen wanted to deny his assertion, but in all honesty, she could not. Mark was a smaller image of his father. It was an unalterable fact. Karen could even understand why Judith had favored Mark from the instant she had looked into his face. Judith had seen her only child all over again in the infant. In all fairness, Karen acknowledged how very hard Judith had worked at being impartial. Staring into her son's eyes,

Karen also acknowledged the near-impossibility of deceiving a bright child. An intelligent, sensitive child saw through the adult games with laser sharpness. At odd, weak moments, Karen had wondered exactly who was leading whom along the path labeled life—the adult or the child?

In possession of far more questions than answers, Karen merely stared at her son in aching despair.

Rand's smile forgave his grandmother, exonerated his brother and complimented Karen. "It's okay, Mom," he said, shrugging off her concern. "I don't mind looking more like you." His smile grew into a grin, revealing the man yet to come. His voice lowered dramatically. "You look like a sizzling sex poodle."

It was altogether improper. It was the wrong time and most assuredly the wrong place, but Karen couldn't help herself; she burst out laughing.

"A sizzling sex poodle?" She fought to compose herself. "Randolf Charles Mitchell, where in the world did you pick up that expression?"

"Around." Rand smirked.

Karen shook her head. Around. Around whom? She couldn't help but wonder, yet she wasn't sure she wanted to know. Nevertheless, she was on the verge of launching into the time-honored parental third degree when two men pushed through the heavy doors leading to the coronary unit. Their appearance wiped her mind of all but thoughts of Charles. Springing from the chair she'd perched on, Karen reached out to grasp Rand's hand. Her eyes darted from one man to the other before settling on Charles's father.

"Randolf?" Her voice held a strained mixture of hope and fear. "How is—"

"Better," Randolf answered before she could finish the question. "The attack wasn't as severe as originally feared." With a smile relieving the taut lines of worry on his face, he crossed the tiled floor to gather Karen and Rand into his arms.

"Grandpa?" The budding man had once again deserted the boy; Rand's tone pleaded for further reassurance. "He's not gonna—" he gulped audibly "—Dad's not gonna die, is he?"

"No, son, your father is not going to die." The authoritative answer came from the man beside Randolf. "I expressly told him I would not permit it." The doctor's compassionate smile contrasted with his stern tone. "It's bad for my image, you know."

Confusion flickered in Rand's brown eyes. The confusion gave way to understanding, which surrendered to appreciation. Rand's grin was back in place, accompanied by a suspicious brightness in his eyes. "Can we see him now?" he asked.

"Yes, you may—"

"Mom?" Mark's squeaked call interrupted the doctor. "Mom?" Sheer thirteen-year-old terror whispered through his lips.

"He's all right, honey." Stepping away from Randolf, Karen extended her hand, silently urging him to release his death grip on his grandmother's hand and join them. "The doctor has just told us your dad is better."

Mark's face crumpled, and he began to sob. Karen moved, but as he had earlier, Rand moved faster.

"Hey, Weepin' Willie, did ya hear that?" Much like his grandfather moments before, Rand gathered his brother into his arms. "Dad's gonna be okay." While stroking Mark's arm with one hand, Rand used his free hand to deliver a gentle punch to his brother's other arm. "Will you lighten up? Mom's nearly out of tissues."

"Besides which," Karen said, gently prying Mark from Rand's amazingly fierce embrace, "the doctor said we may go in to see your dad, and you don't want him to see you crying, do you?"

"No." Mark sniffed. "Can we go now?"

"In a moment," the doctor said. "But first let me brief you." As he'd expected, he received immediate attention. "Your mother is quite right, young man." He smiled at Mark. "You don't want your father to see you crying. It might upset him, and though his condition is much improved, he must not be stressed." His gaze shifted to Karen. "The preliminary test results are favorable. The attack was a warning, and though I won't go into detail at this time, I will tell you it was a warning that must not be treated lightly." Pausing, he stared steadily into Karen's eyes.

Karen experienced a shivery sensation of intuition or premonition; she wasn't sure which it was, but she didn't appreciate either. She wanted to shake her head in repudiation of whatever it was she felt. However, pinned by the doctor's intent regard, she nodded.

Satisfied, the doctor smiled. "Now then," he said briskly, returning his gaze to the boys. "I must urge you not to be frightened by your father's appearance. He is a very sick man, and it shows. Also," he continued, unperturbed when Mark blanched, "I don't want you to be alarmed by the assortment of machines and tubes attached to him. Though they are somewhat uncomfortable, they are necessary.'' He raised his heavy eyebrows. "Do you think you can handle it?"

"Yes, sir," Rand said at once.

"Yes, sir," Mark echoed, if waveringly.

The strength of his smile eased the strain on both boys' faces. "Good." He nodded sharply. "Now, regulations allow only two visitors at a time, but in this instance I will countermand the rules." He looked at Karen. "Ms. Mitchell, you may take your sons in to their father for ten minutes, no longer."

"Very well." Grasping one of each of the boy's hands, Karen moved to obey. She halted when he continued to speak.

"I will consult with you later, while Randolf and Judith are visiting Charles."

The chill of premonition shivered through Karen again. For one instant, rebellion sparked. Then the spark died, and she nodded once more. "Of course, Doctor." She managed to meet his eyes; she even managed a faint smile. He returned the smile, then escorted her and the boys into the coronary unit and to the door of Charles's room. As she crossed the threshold, Karen heard him give instructions to the nurse hovering near the door.

At the sight of his father, looking pasty and gray against the white pillow, Mark began to tremble; Karen could feel the tremors ripple the length of his arm and through the hand clasped in hers. Rand sucked in one sharp breath. A cry of denial rose to her own suddenly unsteady lips.

Look what we've got for you:

. . . A FREE compact umbrella
. . . plus a sampler set of 4 terrific
Silhouette Special Edition® novels,
specially selected by our editors.

5 FREE GIFTS

. . . PLUS a surprise mystery gift
that will delight you.

FREE MYSTERY GIFT

All this just for trying our preview service!

With your trial, you'll get SNEAK PREVIEWS
to 6 new Silhouette Special Edition® novels a
month—before they're available in stores—with
9% off retail on any books you keep (just $2.49
each)—plus 69¢ postage and handling per shipment.

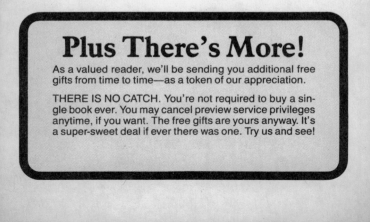

Plus There's More!

As a valued reader, we'll be sending you additional free
gifts from time to time—as a token of our appreciation.

THERE IS NO CATCH. You're not required to buy a single book ever. You may cancel preview service privileges
anytime, if you want. The free gifts are yours anyway. It's
a super-sweet deal if ever there was one. Try us and see!

This could not be Charles Mitchell! The protest rang in her mind in a loud attempt to refute the evidence before her stricken eyes. This man who appeared so lifeless, so bloodless, in no way resembled the Charles Mitchell she knew and had once loved! Everything vital inside Karen rejected the validity of this man's identity. The man himself confirmed it.

"Karen?"

Having believed him asleep, Karen started. The voice was not—and yet strangely was—the voice she remembered. Her fingers tightening convulsively on her sons' hands, she walked to the side of the bed.

"Yes, Charles." With a tiny part of her mind, Karen recognized that her voice was not the same, either.

"Thank you for coming." Charles moved slightly, restlessly. The movement brought the boys into focus. "Rand, Mark?" A smile feathered his pale lips.

"Yes, Dad?" Rand's voice cracked just a little.

"Daddy?" Mark whimpered for a word of assurance.

Even ill, there was no way Charles could miss the abject fear his sons were feeling. For an instant, he appeared mildly annoyed, as if put-upon. Then a hint of compassion flicked in his eyes, and his lips twisted into a wry smile.

"Helluva way to get sprung from school, isn't it, guys?"

By the time she crawled into bed near midnight, Karen felt as if she'd been awake for a solid week. A variation on a tired joke ran persistently through her equally tired brain.

I spent a week one day sitting in a hospital with an ex-mate.

Ta da dum dum.

Muffling a sob, Karen buried her face in the unfamiliar pillow. Jokes. She longed to rant and rave and wail in frustration, and her weary mind was recounting jokes.

The midnight quiet was shattered by the trill of a giggle. Her eyes widening, Karen flopped onto her back and clapped her hand over her mouth. She was giggling! The thought contained an edge of hysteria. She was giggling, for God's sake! Grown-up women didn't giggle! Babies giggled; teenagers giggled! Mature adults did not giggle!

I don't want him in my home!

The silent protest screamed in Karen's head and defined the reason her mind was skipping along the edge of hysteria. She was tired—no, she was emotionally exhausted. Her response had been a delayed reaction to everything that had happened, beginning with Judith's phone call the previous morning and ending with her astonishing consultation with the heart specialist, Dr. Rayburn.

The good doctor had given her a concise description of Charles's present condition based on his examination of both patient and tests. In the doctor's opinion, the attack had been a definite warning. He had then concluded on a note of hesitant optimism for the future. Karen's tension had eased and she had been beginning to relax when the doctor had tossed a verbal bomb at her. Karen was still reeling from the explosive reverberations.

As clearly as if he were standing beside her bed, Karen could hear the even tone of Dr. Rayburn's voice, relaying to her Charles's suggestion that he could recuperate very well in her house in Maine. Now, as then, she cried out in protest.

"No!"

Karen's cry in the quiet room had as much effect as it had earlier in the small consulting room in the hospital. The doctor had offered her a chiding smile and a full measure of disapproval.

"Surely you would not deny your husband the ideal location in which to get well?"

The doctor's softly spoken charge echoed inside her head.

"Charles is not my husband," she had retorted immediately, reminded of the fact that Ben Rayburn was not only a physician but a close friend of the Mitchell family.

"But he is still the father of your children."

It was an irrefutable fact; there was no argument against his statement. "Yes, of course," Karen conceded. "But—"

Rayburn verbally closed in for the kill. "Don't you agree that the boys would feel relieved to know that their father is safely installed under your roof and under your care?"

"But what about Charles's parents?" Karen had demanded, recalling the comfort of the elder Mitchells' spacious suburban home and the guest room she now occupied. "Won't they want him close by?"

"Perhaps." The doctor's smile was too wise, and wry with understanding. "But Randolf is still very actively involved with his company, and Judith,

though charming, is frankly quite helpless in a sickroom situation.'' He smiled again. ''As I'm sure you
know.''

Having had firsthand experience, Karen did know
how very useless Judith was in an emergency. Against
her will, Karen had relived the time Rand had been
thrown from his first two-wheeled bike. Karen had
been at her shop, Charles had been out of town, Judith had been baby-sitting. Karen would never forget
the sheer panic in Judith's voice when she'd called,
begging Karen to tell her what to do. As calmly as
possible, Karen had advised Judith to get Rand to the
hospital, while assuring the older woman that she'd
meet her there to take over. Karen had arrived at the
hospital to find a pale but calm Rand and a devas-
tated Judith.

Oh, yes. Karen knew exactly how useless Judith was
in a sickroom situation. She had had little option but
to nod her head, both in agreement with Dr. Rayburn
and in defeat. Should she remain steadfast in her refusal to house Charles while he recuperated from the
effects of the attack, and her sons learned of her refusal—which they most definitely would—they would
never forgive her. Karen knew that she was well and
truly trapped. She might, and did, rail silently against
Charles for placing her in such an untenable position,
but she had no choice but to offer him succor.

The deed was done; the plans were formulated.
Upon release from the hospital, Charles would ac-
company Karen back to her home in Maine where, it
was fervently agreed upon by all but Karen, he should
fare well in the quiet atmosphere.

Now, hours later, Karen wanted to scream her frustration aloud. She was literally surrounded by people, yet she was very much alone. Unlike the night before, her bed was cold and empty.

Karen moved restlessly; she couldn't, wouldn't, think about the night before. Remembering Paul's fiercely tender possession would only undermine her dwindling store of strength, and she needed her strength for the days and weeks ahead. Yes, she wanted to scream her frustration, but she wouldn't. She was too tired, too susceptible, too close to tears. And she couldn't afford to give in to tears because she feared that if she allowed herself to start crying she might wail the house down.

But in the midnight quiet of the guest room in her former in-laws' home, with her children asleep in the room next to hers, Karen silently cried out in protest and desperation.

Paul.

Oh, fool! she chastened herself mutely. *Why did you refuse his plea to come to you in Boston?*

"Dammit!"

The edgy sound of his own voice echoing back at him, Paul tossed the tangled covers aside and sprang from the unfamiliar motel-room bed that had afforded him precious little relaxation or rest. The bed was not at fault. Indeed, the bed was firm and comfortable—but Paul wasn't. He was not firm in his conviction that he was doing the right thing by leaving Karen, nor was he comfortable with the miles now separating them.

Paul was hurting, in his mind and in his body. With wry self-understanding, he acknowledged that, were Karen there to share the bed with him, the unfamiliar mattress would offer sweet surcease to his active imagination and too long denied, and now starving, flesh.

Into his tired mind danced a vision of her the night before, passionate, laughing, as hungry for him as he was for her. His body throbbing with a demand that could not be appeased, Paul muttered a curse.

Paul needed Karen, not merely in the physical sense but in every way there was. He needed her laughter as well as her impassioned murmurs. He needed her levelheadedness as well as her physical abandon. He needed her spiritually as well as physically. And the need had been growing with each successive mile as more distance came between them.

Pulling a robe over his chilled, naked body, Paul paced the inhibiting confines of the room and wished for a drink—a double. By itself, his thirst was sure sign of his mental condition. Paul rarely drank hard liquor, and then only in moderation. His tastes ran more to cool white wine and coolheadedness. Paul had not been handed his reputation as a shrewd banker and businessman; he had gained it by intelligent hard work. In his opinion, intelligence and indulgence did not coexist profitably. Nevertheless, at midnight in a lonely motel room in Connecticut, Paul wished he had a large measure of something potent and mind-divorcing.

In keen anticipation, he picked up the room-service menu. He sighed, acceptance replacing anticipation as he noted that room service was available only until eleven at night. Flipping the menu onto the desk-dresser, Paul resumed pacing.

How had it happened? he mused, cursing softly when his shinbone made painful contact with a corner of the bed. Ignoring the scrape, he concentrated on the question he'd asked himself.

How had it happened, this uncomfortable, unnerving state he now found himself in? Paul shook his head. He had exchanged a few innocuous remarks with a stranger on the beach. And from that most innocent of beginnings, he now found himself needing that stranger as a scholar needed books, as an addict needed a fix—merely to exist. But why?

Paul frowned. Why, indeed, this one particular woman? What was so special about Karen that made her different, at least to him, from countless others? And Paul had met countless other women, both socially and professionally. Yet not one of those other women had been able to catch his personal interest, although, modesty aside, he had been aware of how very hard a number of them had tried to capture his attention.

What made Karen special? Coming to an abrupt stop in the center of the room, Paul gazed blankly at the rumpled bed while he peered inward, seeking answers.

There had been an instantaneous attraction between them, he recalled, feeling a tiny thrill at the memory of her smiling up at him from her seated position in the sand. But Paul was well aware that there was more to the way he was feeling than could be explained as simple physical or chemical attraction.

Perhaps it was Karen's levelheadedness and stability that appealed to him. Paul conceded the possibility; after the years he'd spent attempting to deal with a rather unstable woman, that quality would appeal to him. But, he reasoned, there was much more involved here than mere levelheadedness and stability.

Perhaps it was Karen's warmth and generous spirit that charmed him. A faint smile tipped up the corners of Paul's lips. Yes, he had been most decidedly charmed by her warmth and spirit, especially since both attributes had been sorely lacking in his wife. But warmth and spirit didn't quite encompass all he was feeling, either.

Perhaps it was simply that Karen was, without question, a natural, down-to-earth, real person, meeting life on her own terms, with her own methods.

Into Paul's mind crept a vision of her large, outdated house, standing foursquare before the winds raking the land and the storms flung from the sea.

Paul smiled and sighed.

Karen Mitchell was like the house she had chosen to retreat to after the failure of her marriage. With a smile on her lips and a defiant toss of her head, she had deserted the excitement of the city to stand foursquare on ancestral earth. With her principles intact, Karen lived the only way she knew how to live, embracing the moralistic doctrine that Paul knew was tormenting her conscience because of her abandon in his arms.

A spasm of pain and sadness flickered over Paul's face. He knew there was no way Karen could rationalize a contradiction. He was also certain that, to her way of thinking, giving herself to him had been a contradiction of every one of her beliefs, regardless of the pleasure and satisfaction derived from her act of giving. Karen's self-recrimination had been her reason for rejecting his suggestion that he follow her to Boston.

Her rejection was the reason for the way he was hurting at that moment. Karen Mitchell, with her laughter and passion, her spirit and inhibiting fears, was the one person in the world that Paul Vanzant needed and ached for.

He needed her. His chest heaving with a deeply indrawn breath, Paul tossed off his robe and slid into the empty bed.

He needed her, not only in his bed but in his life, as well. And whether or not she acknowledged it, Paul instinctively knew that Karen needed him, too. All he had to do was convince her of her need.

"Dammit!"

Chapter Eight

I need him!

The cry stabbed into Karen's tired mind with increasingly depressing regularity. With each passing mile that brought them closer to the large house on the coast of Maine, Karen's thoughts persisted in conjuring up visions of the one person she didn't want to think about.

Where was he? Was he at home with his son and daughter-in-law in Philadelphia, or was he wandering again in search of whatever or whomever? It hurt Karen to think about it—to think about him. Still, weary after two weeks' vigilance at Charles's bedside, at the hospital and then in his parents' home, she could not stem the flow of conjecture.

Paul.

Forming his name, even silently, relieved a bit of the tension coiling along her nerves. The commitment to have Charles in her home to recuperate had been made. Karen would abide by it, even if she was secretly resentful of the imposition. For while she might have held out against Dr. Rayburn and the elder Mitchells, she had caved in to the pleas of her children. She would play nursemaid to Charles, but her thoughts were her own. And Karen's thoughts were all on Paul Vanzant and her need to see him, talk to him, simply be with him.

Deep in thought, Karen was only marginally aware of her passenger, surrounded by luggage on the back seat of her car. Alert to her wandering attention, Charles made his presence known with a soft but audible groan. His ploy worked beautifully; Karen snapped to attention.

"Charles, are you all right?" Her gaze sought his in the rearview mirror.

"Yes, I guess so." Charles met her probing stare for an instant. "I'm just getting a little tired." His eyelids drooped. "It's been a long day."

Karen felt contrite immediately. Charles's mild complaint was valid; it had been a long day, and it wasn't over yet.

"Would you like me to stop somewhere?" she asked anxiously, chancing another quick glance at the mirror. "You could have a warm drink and stretch your legs."

"Yes...if you don't mind." His voice was little more than a weary whisper.

Alarm raced through Karen, chilling her body, momentarily freezing her mind. What would she do if he became ill? The road was virtually deserted, with few roadside stops. If Charles became ill, or had another attack . . . ! Karen caught her thoughts up short. She was beginning to panic, and there was no reason for it. Hadn't Dr. Rayburn approved the trip? Surely if the doctor had thought there was any danger to Charles, he wouldn't have hesitated to state his objections. But the doctor hadn't objected. In fact, Dr. Rayburn had heartily approved.

Bolstered by the memory of the specialist's endorsement of Charles's plea to be allowed to leave Boston sooner than originally planned, Karen brought her fears under control. It would be all right, she assured herself. Charles would be all right. He was tired, understandably so, and that was all. But the arduous trip would be over before too long—thank heaven!

Karen drew a deep, calming breath. "I don't mind at all," she said, smiling into the mirror. "I could use a drink and a stretch myself." Her gaze drifted back to the road. "I'll stop at the next restaurant or diner."

They drove in silence for some fifteen minutes, and Karen was beginning to wonder if he had fallen asleep when Charles drew her attention to the golden arches rising above the highway in the distance. Nodding her acceptance of the fast-food restaurant, Karen slowed the car to make the turn into the spacious parking lot.

Though the late-fall air was cool, the sun had an Indian-summer warmth. After stepping from the car, Charles stood still, inhaling deep, reviving breaths of the autumn air.

"I missed the foliage," he said, strolling beside her toward the restaurant. "I was involved in a project, too busy to notice the change of seasons."

Karen didn't respond; she couldn't think of a thing to say to his remark. For as long as she could remember, Charles had always been too involved with some project or other—or, as she had later learned, with some woman or other—to take much notice of the seasonal changes.

While Karen went to the counter to purchase regular coffee for herself and decaffeinated coffee for him, Charles chose a table on the outdoor patio. He was standing in the sunlight by the brick enclosure, his profile to her, as Karen carried the steaming cups out to the open-air section of the restaurant. Her gaze remote, detached, Karen studied the man she had at one time loved above all others.

Charles hadn't changed much in the five years since their divorce. Except for a slightly drawn look and a grayish pallor in his cheeks, evidence of the heart attack he'd suffered, his appearance was the same. He was still an extremely attractive, dynamic-looking man. Above average in height, his body scrupulously toned by rigorous workouts, Charles was undeniably a handsome man. In addition to his exceptional looks, Charles's personality, and his masculine approach, had always set female hearts fluttering. And at age twenty, Karen had been no exception.

But Karen was no longer twenty and no longer quite as naive as she'd been when meeting Charles for the first time. Then she had been literally swept off her feet by him. Now, older, wiser and much more discerning, Karen, though moved to compassion by his recent ordeal, was completely unmoved by the attractive picture he presented bathed by sparkling fall sunshine.

"Careful, it's hot," she advised, handing him the Styrofoam cup. Tentatively sipping her own coffee, Karen gazed out over the waist-high patio enclosure. A faint smile tugged at her lips as her glance came to rest on a small play area, provided by the management for children restless from traveling.

It seemed to Karen that it had been a long time since her own boys had derived entertainment from the simple pleasure of a short ride down a slide or balancing on a teeter-totter. A soft sigh eased through her lips as, in her mind's eye, she saw her sons' bright faces as they laughed and begged her to push their swings higher and higher.

Suddenly Karen missed Rand and Mark, more acutely than at any other time since the divorce, and she ached to see them, touch them, hold them in her arms as she had the day of their arrival at the hospital. That unforgettable day was now two-week-old history. Randolf had escorted the boys back to school the day after the assortment of tubes and monitoring machines had been removed from their father and Charles had been moved from the coronary unit to a regular hospital room. On that day, in the midst of the relief displayed by Charles and his family, Karen had felt deserted by her sons, and she still felt deserted. Staring at the children's brightly colored playthings, Karen blinked against a rush of tears.

Apparently the play area also brought thoughts of the boys to Charles's mind. "Did I tell you I spoke to Rand and Mark on the phone before we left Boston this morning?" he asked in a murmur.

His question dried the gathering tears and drew her frowning gaze to his watchful eyes. "No." Karen shook her head. "Why did you call them?"

Charles moved his shoulders in a half shrug. "They were both so reluctant to return to school—" he shrugged again "—I thought I'd reassure them about the state of my health."

"And were they reassured?"

"Seemed to be." Charles paused to smile. "But it's difficult to tell with kids, isn't it?"

"Yes." Karen returned his smile, sharing with him, if nothing else, concern for the well-being of the children they had created together. "Children have a tendency to talk tough when they're frightened. And your attack frightened them very badly."

"And what about you? Were you frightened, too?" Charles gave her his most intense, melting look.

Immune to his charm, Karen didn't melt; she merely smiled. "Yes, Charles," she admitted, deliberately pandering to his need for an ego boost. "I was frightened." Her smile grew wry. "I have no wish for your demise."

"I'm glad to hear it. Knowing you were frightened gives me hope for the weeks ahead."

For an instant, Karen went absolutely still, barely breathing, afraid to think. But she had to know, had to ask. "What do you mean?" She had to force her fingers to ease their grip on the cup. "What are you getting at?"

His expression was one of superiority; Karen had always detested that particular expression. Now she discovered she resented it as well. "Don't smirk at me,

Charles," she snapped. "Just explain what you meant by your remark."

Annoyance flickered across his face, revealing his dissatisfaction with her response. Karen could read his expression as easily as a first-grade primer. Always before, when she had been young and fathoms-deep in love, she had quailed at his mildest expression of reproof, quailed and hastened to appease him. Karen was no longer young or fathoms-deep in love with Charles. She no longer quailed at much of anything, and she couldn't have cared less if he was appeased or not. His expression made it evident that he was not thrilled with the mature Karen.

"You do realize that the boys are hoping for a reconciliation between us while I'm recuperating in your home," he finally replied in an infuriatingly condescending tone. "Don't you?"

"A reconciliation!" Karen exclaimed, stunned. "But it's been five years! Why would either one of them think—" Her voice lost substance, and she shook her head as if trying to clear her mind. "That's absolutely ridiculous!"

"Why is it?" Charles retorted, his features betraying annoyance and anger.

"Why?" In her shock, Karen failed to notice the renewed strength underlying his tone. "Charles, we have been divorced over five years. Of course the idea of a reconciliation between us is ridiculous."

"And I say it isn't," he insisted mulishly. "We're both older, mature, more inclined to accept responsibility," he went on doggedly.

Karen couldn't believe what she was hearing. She was forced to stifle the temptation to demand:

"What's this 'we' bit? I accepted the responsibility of marriage from day one." Instead, she attacked from a different direction. "And what about your latest, er, friend?" she asked sweetly, recalling the svelte, ambitious blonde he'd introduced her to the last time Karen had taken the boys to visit their grandparents in Boston. "Don't you think she—ah, what was her name again?—oh, yes, Claudia, wasn't it?" His lips had tightened in growing anger, but Karen went on ruthlessly. "Whatever. Don't you think *she* might object?"

"Yes, her name is Claudia," Charles said in a tight voice. "And whether she objects or not doesn't matter. She doesn't matter. The important thing here is—"

"To get home before nightfall," Karen interrupted to finish for him. "This subject is irrelevant," she continued impatiently, tossing her empty cup into a trash can, "and closed." She spun away from him.

"The subject is not irrelevant," Charles argued, following her at a leisurely pace to the car. "And will be reopened again when you're in a more receptive frame of mind."

Don't hold your breath, Karen thought, sliding behind the wheel and slamming the car door forcefully.

Throughout the remainder of the trip, the only voice to break the silence came from the car radio, which Karen had switched on before driving out of the restaurant's parking area. But inside her head, her thoughts seethed and popped like an untended stew coming to a boil.

How dare he? she railed silently. How dare Charles Mitchell assume that he had but to smile and snap his

fingers to bring her to heel like a trained pet? And how
dare he as casually dismiss his current paramour as not
mattering? What had Claudia ever done to deserve his
disdainful dismissal? Karen asked herself furiously.
Come to that, what had Karen Mitchell ever done to
earn his dubious favor?

Anger and tension gnawing at her, Karen arrived
home exhausted and in a chancy temper. Tipped off
to her mood by either her expression or her defiantly
angled jaw, Charles prudently offered no resistance
when she suggested they have a light supper, then re-
tire for the night.

"I'll take the room across the hall from yours," he
said between sips of the canned vegetable soup she had
heated for their meal.

A protest sprang immediately to Karen's lips; the
room across the hall from her belonged to Paul! Biting her lip, she caught back the declaration before it
spilled from her tongue. A sense of despair filled her
at the realization that the room did not belong to Paul
and that it was doubtful he would ever occupy it again.
Still, it grated on her to know that Charles would be
sleeping in the bed that had supported Paul's body. As
she opened her mouth to suggest he choose another
room, Charles effectively silenced her.

"I want to be as close to you as possible," he said
in a tone that held a hint of fear and uncertainty. His
hand moved in an absent way to lightly brush his
chest. "I need to know you'll hear me if I call for you
during the night."

What could she say? Karen thought bleakly. How
could she possibly deny him the assurance of having
her within calling distance in the night in the event he

suffered another— She cut off the unthinkable consideration with a sharp, brief shake of her head. She had no choice, she told herself, forcing a smile to her lips for him. And anyway, it was really only a room, an empty room. Paul was long gone from it.

"Of course, you may have any room you like." Karen's smile faltered as she glanced up, catching the gleam of speculation Charles quickly banished from his watchful eyes. "It'll only take me a minute to put fresh sheets on the bed." As she moved to get up, his hand shot across the table to capture hers. His action was too similar to Paul's motion of a few weeks earlier to be comfortable. Yet the action produced a different reaction in Karen. With Paul, her urge had been to turn her hand and entwine her fingers in his, but with Charles, she had to fight an impulse to snatch her hand away.

"There's no need to rush," he said, smiling at her as he gently squeezed her hand. "You've been driving all day. Relax and enjoy the rest of your soup. Join me in a cup of coffee."

"It's decaffeinated." Karen made a face.

Charles laughed. "It's really not that bad once you get used to it."

The way having him in her home wouldn't be that bad once she got used to it? Karen wondered, carefully sliding her hand from beneath his. In connection with that thought, an oft-repeated saying of her grandfather's sprang into Karen's mind.

A body can get used to most anything, even hanging if'n it hangs long enough.

Was that to be her life-style for who knew how many weeks or months—getting used to having

Charles in her home, being constantly at his beck and call? The prospect was more than a little daunting. Deciding it just might be easier to get used to hanging, Karen got up to get the coffee.

When finally, after keeping Charles company for over an hour, then briskly changing the sheets on the guest room bed, Karen was free to seek the privacy of her own room, she did so with mounting trepidation. In truth, her room was not at all private. It was occupied by the unsubstantial, yet very real, presence of Paul Vanzant.

Long-denied memories crowding in on her, Karen quickly showered, pulled on a nightgown and slipped beneath the covers on her bed. She was cold and shivering, but her physical condition had little to do with the plunging temperature outside and everything to do with the sense of Paul permeating her mind. Paul was there, in her room with her, whether she wanted him there or not.

Karen fiercely fought against the sensation of being completely taken over by the lingering essence that was Paul, but she was swiftly immersed in thoughts of the last night they had spent together in that room, in her bed.

Seeing him clearly, feeling as if she had but to reach out to touch him, Karen saw Paul as he'd looked that last night as he'd silently stalked across the room to her, his eyes dark with intent, his firm jaw set in a determined thrust, his finely sculpted lips curved seductively.

A thrill of anticipation crept the length of her spine, and Karen felt again the breathless excitement she'd experienced at being swept into his arms before being tossed onto the bed. Karen's breathing grew shallow, and her eyes slowly drifted shut in surrender. The gates of memory flew open, releasing a heady rush of sweet remembrance. Paul was with her, beside her on the bed, within her—masterful, demanding, forceful and gentle with her by turns. And she was his, a wanton flame burning solely to illuminate his world. Their fire had burned through the night, leaping higher and higher until, near dawn, they had burned each other into emotionally charred exhaustion. Karen's soul still felt the sting of Paul's searing possession.

A stab of pain shattered the illusion of her wakeful dream. Moaning a protest against encroaching reality, Karen opened her eyes and concentrated on the source of her discomfort. The pain shot along her rigid fingers, cramped from gripping the bedding. With a sigh, Karen consciously relaxed her fingers and her body and her mind.

Paul was gone.

She was alone.

In her sorrow, Karen completely forgot the man sleeping in the room directly across from her own.

Paul was gone.

Was she back in Maine?

The thought came out of nowhere to break Paul's concentration. Exhaling a harsh sigh, he straightened his cramped back and pulled the oversize silver-rimmed glasses off to massage the bridge of his nose. Paul was tired. He was working too hard and sleeping too little. He knew it. He didn't particularly care.

It was November. It was cold. It was past midnight. The Thanksgiving holiday was three days away,

Paul didn't particularly care about any of those facts, either.

Upon returning to Philadelphia in October, Paul had thrown himself into his work. Not the business of banking—he had retired from that and intended to remain retired from it. The business Paul had immersed himself in was a small company he'd acquired before his wife's sudden, unexpected death. At the time, the small company had been in financial trouble and floundering badly under inept management. Paul had taken over the company with the sole intent of dismantling it and selling it off piecemeal, thereby deriving a profit. After the shock of his wife's death, Paul had put off the order to begin the process of tearing down the failing company, thus allowing the business to continue on its stumbling course.

During the months following his wife's death, Paul had brushed aside his son's advice to either drop the ax on the company or take it on himself and whip it into shape, as Peter himself had done so successfully with his own wife's struggling company.

Paul had been back in Philadelphia less than a week, drifting through life like a soul in search of a body, when Peter had again made the suggestion that his father take an active hand in the small company. Peter's cool, offhand suggestion had been a godsend.

Seeking purpose, any purpose other than eating his foolish, middle-aged heart out over a woman, Paul acted on Peter's suggestion by investigating the company's possibilities. Very little time was required for Paul to reach the conclusion that, with applied intelligence and a lot of hard work, the company could not only be salvaged but made to show a profit. Paul had been applying both intelligence and hard work since then.

His efforts were beginning to show results, Paul acknowledged, both on the company's books and in his own thin, drawn face. The thought of his appearance brought a grimace to his lips. It would be some time before the small company was humming along and returning a creditable profit, but Paul, with little else to occupy himself with, was in no particular hurry. He had all the time in the world to steer the company into becoming viable—if he lived through the self-punishment of forgetfulness through work.

Forgetfulness. Paul's fingers curled into a fist. There wasn't enough work in the world to give him forgetfulness. How he longed to be able to close his eyes, just once, without seeing Karen, hearing Karen, needing Karen. Her face teased his memory. Her laughter haunted him. The thrill of her passion tormented his body.

Having allowed the thought of her into his conscious mind, Paul envisioned Karen back in the house on the Maine coast, back in the house and back in the bed they had shared that last night. His body tightened painfully as he relived the sweetness of Karen's surrender, felt again the thrill of possessing her, being possessed by her.

The very intensity of his feelings made Paul uneasy, and with grim determination he banished the memories from his mind.

What in the world was the matter with him? The question was almost like an old friend, so familiar was it to him.

He had been confused and angry most of the time since he'd returned home, and he still was. That condition was another old friend.

Could he possibly be experiencing a delayed midlife crisis? Paul frowned. This consideration was completely new and unexpected. He voiced his opinion of midlife crises, delayed or otherwise, with a muttered, pithy curse.

Well, then, what the hell was the matter with him? Paul's smile was extremely wry. He was pining for a woman, that was what was the matter with him. And he didn't know quite how to handle his jumbled emotions.

Lord! Paul thought, raking a hand through his hair. How could he possibly know how to handle these unfamiliar emotions; he had never felt this way before. The realization stilled his fingers. Paul's hand fell to the desk unnoticed.

He had never felt this way before! Not even with his wife, the beautiful Carolyn, had he experienced quite this intensity of emotional upheaval, this need, this want, this consuming desire to simply *be* with another person!

Was Karen back in Maine?

Probably.

Then why was he in Pennsylvania?

Because she rejected your offer to be with her.

A sharp burst of humorless laughter broke the silence in the dimly lighted study. Suddenly impatient with the work he'd been straining his eyes over, with himself, with questions that hurt and answers that hurt even more, Paul shoved back his chair and rose to prowl around the solid oak desk.

Restless, dissatisfied, he paced to the bookshelves, only to pivot around again without glancing at a single title on the leather spines. He directed his course to a short black-leather-padded wet bar at the opposite end of the room. He was tipping a bottle over a wide squat glass when his hand was arrested by a drawling voice.

"If you're playing bartender, you can splash some of that Scotch into a glass for me."

Tilting his head, Paul peered at his son over the rims of his glasses. His impeccable business suit enhancing the muscular slenderness of his tall body, Peter stood in the study doorway, one shoulder propped indolently against the frame.

"On the rocks or straight up?" Paul asked dryly.

"I'm driving." Shrugging, Peter pushed himself away from the frame and strolled to the bar to grin at his father. "I'll have two ice cubes and a large dash of seltzer."

Paul's lips twisted with distaste. "A helluva thing to do to aged Scotch," he muttered, dropping two ice cubes into the glass, then drowning both whiskey and ice with seltzer. After handing the glass to his son, Paul raised his in a salute. "What shall we drink to?"

Peter's darkly handsome face took on a speculative expression, and his dark eyes began to glitter behind narrowed lids. "Let's see," he said, drawing his brows together in a frown. "We could drink to the future success of your new toy, but I think that's assured now, considering the killing amount of work you've put into it."

"Peter." A hint of warning sounded in Paul's voice as he recognized the edge in his son's voice; Peter was about to go for his father's throat—figuratively speaking.

"Or we could drink to your health," Peter went on, ignoring his father's warning tone. "But that's in some doubt, considering the amount of work you've put into that company."

"Peter." The note in Paul's tone was no longer a hint; it was a full-fledged warning to back off and shut up.

"Then again," Peter continued, unperturbed by the parental censure, "we could drink to the woman—whoever she is." Raising his glass to his lips, Peter took a sip of the Scotch while closely watching his father's face for a reaction.

Though he tried his damnedest, Paul didn't disappoint his son; a muscle jerked along his clenched jaw.

"Is she pretty, Dad?" Peter asked softly. "Are you in love with her?"

Chapter Nine

Karen, where are my gray slacks?"

With a flicker of annoyance moving over her set lips, Karen sighed and shut her eyes. Gray slacks. Where were they? She had pressed them earlier that morning—and then she'd hung them in his closet.

"Have you looked in your closet?"

"Yes, of course, but . . . Oh, here they are. Sorry."

Yes, so am I. Karen didn't allow herself to think any further about how very sorry she was about many things, starting with her concession to the request to have Charles recuperate in her home and ending with Charles recuperating in her home. She didn't have time to think about it. There was simply too much to do. She glanced at the kitchen clock and smothered a groan. The boys would be home for the holiday weekend soon—picked up at school and delivered to her by their grandparents. A second groan escaped her. Impatience danced along her nerves.

Why had she allowed Charles to talk her into invit- -ing his parents to visit for the weekend? Karen grimaced. She knew precisely why she'd given in to his request; Charles had simply worn her down with pleas and promises of how wonderful it would be to have an old-fashioned family gathering for Thanksgiving. And, as his health had so very obviously improved during his stay with her, Karen hesitated to remind him that they had never gathered as a family for *any* holiday, even in the days when she had still believed they *were* a family. So in the end she had given in, ignoring his smug smile of satisfaction. But now, running behind schedule and distracted by yet another reminder of his ineptitude concerning anything vaguely domestic, even to the point of being unable to find his own slacks in his own closet, Karen was beginning to wonder if all her marbles were rolling around in the proper slots.

Get busy, Karen, she chided herself. Time waits for no man or woman, and there's precious little time to ruminate. Besides, if she did allow herself to think about it, she'd probably start wailing or tearing her hair out of her head. And either way, she'd be a shocking sight for Rand and Mark when they arrived for the Thanksgiving holiday—not to mention Judith and Randolf.

Making a face at her own whimsical thoughts, Karen opened her eyes and glared down at the pie she'd been working on when Charles had distracted her. A sour expression pinched her lips. She hated pumpkin pie. But, as Charles had so gently reminded her, both his parents loved pumpkin pie, and really, what was Thanksgiving without pumpkin pie?

Enjoyable? Karen had not offered the comment at the time of the discussion. She had still been in shock after being informed that she would be entertaining her former in-laws for the holiday.

Now, crimping the edges of the piecrust with more vigor than necessary, Karen fumed in silent frustration. Until Charles had dropped his informational bombshell on her, she had been looking forward to the holiday simply because the boys would be home. She had even considered going out to a restaurant for the traditional meal instead of cooking it herself. Charles's news had ended her pipe dream of being waited on.

The combined scents of pumpkin, ginger and cinnamon tickled Karen's nose as she poured the mixture into the pie shell. A soft smile curved her lips. Too bad the finished product didn't taste as good as it smelled, she mused, sliding the pie onto the center rack in the oven. She was setting the oven timer when Charles sauntered into the kitchen.

"How do I look?" he asked, striking a pose for her.

Experiencing an eerie sense of déjà vu, Karen turned to face him. His pose was much the same as Paul's had been weeks before when he'd breezed into the kitchen after repairing the shutters. Swamped with a longing so intense she felt light-headed for an instant, Karen couldn't speak or even breathe. There before her, in Charles's stead, stood the one person she yearned to see. His aristocratic head was tilted at a quizzical angle, and his beautiful mouth curved teasingly. He was smiling at her, for her, only for her. Karen was forced to grasp the edge of the stove to steady herself, so great was the shaft of pain that sliced into her chest. In despair, she felt every minute of every aching hour she had lived through since driving away from Paul in that restaurant parking lot increasing her loneliness a hundred times over. Her heart, her mind, her body wept with need of him.

Paul.

"Karen?" Charles took a step toward her. "You look so strange. Are you all right?"

Karen blinked and began breathing again. "Yes, of course." She managed a shaky smile to reassure him. "The heat from the oven," she said, improvising. "It made me a little dizzy."

Unconvinced, Charles arched a skeptical brow. "You're pale. Are you sure you're okay?"

"I said I was." Stepping around him, she walked to the sink to rinse the flour off her hands and run cold water over her thundering pulse. Frowning, she stared at the vein throbbing in her wrist. This was ridiculous! Rattled, she flinched when Charles laid a hand on her shoulder.

"I think you'd better sit down." There was a hint of a command in his tone that abraded her nerves.

"I'm all right!"

Karen was suddenly impatient. She was a thirty-seven-year-old mother of two, mooning like a teenager over a man she'd known exactly three days! It had to stop. She could deal with her feelings of guilt over her moral lapse; she couldn't handle a bad case of lovesickness.

Lovesickness? Everything inside Karen went still. Love? A tremor ran down her legs, leaving them weak. Love! Unsteady, quaking inside, she stumbled to a chair, unconsciously obeying Charles's order. Her head whirling, she stared at the homey, domestic-looking clutter of sprinkled flour and baking utensils on the table.

She couldn't be in love!

"Here, sip this."

Karen started and frowned at the small glass Charles shoved into her hand. The pungent aroma of expensive bourbon filled her senses. Frowning, she glanced up at him.

"What's this for?"

"You." Charles's expression was grim. "It'll clear your head."

It'll take more than bourbon. Karen smiled at the thought. Charles thought she was smiling at him, and he smiled back at her.

"Go on," he urged. "Drink it."

Why not? Raising the glass, she sipped and choked on the potent whiskey. Charles laughed. Karen tossed him a wry look.

"Better?"

"Much better," she lied, taking another tiny sip. "My head's clear now." That much was true; Karen felt extremely clearheaded. She wasn't particularly happy with the condition. Mental lucidity brought the truth crashing home.

She was in love with Paul Vanzant!

But acknowledging her emotional condition and living with it were two entirely different matters. She didn't want to be in love with Paul; she didn't want to be in love with anyone.

Standing, Karen began to clear the baking debris from the table. She didn't have time to think about

Paul or about love. She had too much to do. It was the day before Thanksgiving. Her boys were due within the hour. Karen's lips compressed. Her boys *and* her former in-laws were due within the hour, she corrected herself.

Damn! Why did life have to be so complicated?

"You never did answer my question."

Charles's aggrieved tone drew Karen from her fruitless contemplation. Pausing in the act of wiping the flour from the tabletop, she angled her head to frown at him.

"What question was that?"

Standing, he again struck his male-model pose. "How do I look?"

Karen couldn't decide whether to laugh or cry. Charles's self-absorption was beyond belief. She chose to laugh.

"You look like you just stepped off the cover of *GQ*," she said, controlling an urge to roll her eyes. "Very chic," she added, sighing inwardly as he preened visibly, not unlike a strutting peacock. "Very man-about-townish."

In all honesty, Karen had to admit that Charles did, in fact, present an elegant picture of the man on the go relaxing at home for the holiday. His choice of a blue-on-blue silk shirt complemented the hand-tailored gray slacks. His cheeks gleamed with a freshly shaved sheen. His shampooed hair looked squeaky clean. His perfect teeth glistened white in contrast to his sun-lamp-tanned skin. All in all, he made Karen feel unkempt and grubby by comparison.

"I think I'll take a shower." Tossing the dishcloth into the sink, Karen headed for the hallway.

"What about dinner?"

"What about it?" Karen paused in the doorway to slant a challenging look at him.

Charles glanced around the untidy kitchen. "You haven't started it." His frown said more than words. "You do realize that my parents and the boys will be here any time now?"

How could she not realize it? Karen wondered when he persisted in reminding her of it. She hesitated, amazed at her unusual willingness to desert a messy kitchen. Then she shrugged. Realizing that it would keep, she dashed into the hallway.

"I'll get everything together after I've had my shower," she called to him as she started up the stairs. "Meanwhile, you can load the dishwasher and start a fresh pot of coffee."

"Me?"

Karen paused at the top of the stairs, arrested by the note of shock in Charles's tone. His obvious amazement should not have surprised her. Charles had been spoiled all his life, first by his doting mother and then by his equally doting wife. Karen felt positive that every one of his girlfriends, past and present, had continued the tradition of catering to his every murmured whim. No wonder the man had been shocked at being told to load the dishwasher and prepare coffee.

"Never mind, Charles," she called to him. "I'll take care of it when I get back down." Shoulders drooping, she headed for her bedroom, deciding the chances of the relaxed, happy holiday she had envisioned were slim to none.

What kind of holiday celebration would Paul be having?

The thought crept into Karen's unguarded mind, stilling her fingers on her shirt button. A sigh of longing ruffled the quiet of her room.

Paul.

A rush of hot moisture drew a film over Karen's eyes. Then she blinked rapidly and shook her head. She had to stop this! It was not only ridiculous, it was impossible. For a moment out of time, she had stepped beyond the norm to engage in a blazing, thoroughly satisfying love affair. An affair, moreover, that had had precious little to do with love. Now her life was back to its normal, dull routine. The affair was over; her lover was gone. That was that.

Her lecture to herself over, Karen finished undressing and stepped into the shower. The gush of water from the shower drowned out the sound of her whispered plea.

Dear God! I can't be in love with him!

"I had no idea you were such an excellent cook, Patricia." Paul raised his glass in a salute to his daughter-in-law. "My compliments. I'm grateful to you and Peter for insisting I share your Thanksgiving Day meal."

"Thank you, Paul." A delighted smile enhancing her beautiful, aristocratic face, Patricia inclined her head in acceptance of his praise. Then she shattered the elegant illusion by aiming an impish grin at her husband. "Dare we tell your father that you assisted in preparing the meal, darling?"

Peter Vanzant's thin lips eased into a smile of supreme male satisfaction. "We may," he murmured, raising his glass to his mouth to acknowledge his father's toast to Patricia. "But please don't expect a gasp of surprise from Dad." Peter's smile slashed into a grin. "He wields a mean hand at the stove, himself."

"Really!" Patricia actually gaped at her father-in-law.

"I manage." Comfortable in the company of the two younger people, Paul relaxed in the dining room chair.

Peter laughed softly. "He manages very well," he observed in a dry tone. "But I agree, love." His tone had softened to a caress. "The meal was an artistic achievement."

"Give yourself a pat on the back, as well, love." Patricia tilted her glass in a toast to her husband.

Love. Paul controlled an urge to close his eyes—and his ears. He had heard the endearment countless times since his arrival at his son's home several hours earlier. Sipping his wine, Paul gazed at his son and daughter-in-law over the rim of the glass. Peter and Patricia were so obviously in love, and they didn't hesitate to voice the affection they felt for one another. The result of that love was the tiny, beautiful child napping in a cradle in the corner of the dining room.

Concealing a sigh, Paul gazed down at the table and saw another, smaller one set in a windowed alcove off a large, old-fashioned kitchen. Unbidden, his inner gaze skimmed off the edge of the imaginary tabletop to the carpeted floor beneath. His heartbeat accelerating inside his chest, Paul could *see* Karen, her eyes cloudy with passion, her moist lips parted, her arms held out in invitation to him . . . to *him*!

". . . Dad?"

The sound of Peter's voice shattered the illusion. Swallowing a groan, Paul glanced up, a faint, self-mocking smile on his lips. "I'm sorry, I was preoccupied. What did you say?"

A tiny frown line drew Peter's dark brows together. "I asked if you'd care for dessert."

"No." Paul offered Patricia an apologetic smile. "I couldn't possibly eat another bite."

Patricia's nod was gracious. "Perhaps later."

"I—" Paul paused. In that instant, the decision was made. It was not his usual way. Paul rarely made a decision without careful consideration of all the possibilities involved. But this particular decision felt exactly right for him; he would go with it. "I'm afraid I won't be here later. I have something I must do."

"Surely you're not going home to work, Dad?" Peter exclaimed, scowling at the very idea of his father working on a holiday, forgetting that he had done so himself many times in his pre-Patricia days.

Paul raised a hand, palm out in the age-old sign asking for peace. "No, Peter, I am not going home to work." His lips twitched in amused anticipation of Peter's reaction to his next statement. "I'm going home to pack." Peter didn't disappoint him.

"Pack!" Peter's voice was rough with astonishment.

"Pack?" Patricia merely sounded confused.

"As in clothes into suitcases," Peter explained dryly.

"But where are you going?" The question came simultaneously from Paul's host and hostess. Peter answered his own query before his father had a chance to respond. "Are you flying to Texas to see Nicole?"

"No." Paul smiled and shook his head. "I spoke to both Nicole and J.B. this morning, and they are fine." He hesitated only a moment before asking quietly, "Peter, do you remember our conversation the other evening?"

"How could I forget?" Peter grimaced. "As I recall, the conversation was pretty much one-sided—mine. You refused to respond in any way."

"Yes, well—" Paul shrugged "—you must admit, your line of questioning was rather personal."

"What is this all about?" Patricia glanced from her husband to her father-in-law. "What conversation? When?"

Paul was content to stare at Peter until the younger man answered his wife. "I stopped by the house to see Dad after my meeting the other night," he explained tersely. "We had a discussion."

Patricia gave a long-suffering sigh but asked patiently, "A discussion about what?"

Paul continued to stare at Peter; Peter's angular features tightened.

"I'm waiting."

Paul nearly lost control and smiled. Peter sighed in exasperation and defeat.

"I asked Dad if his lady friend was pretty and, er, if he was in love with her."

"Peter, you didn't!" Patricia was visibly appalled at her mate's lack of both manners and tact. "Your father's personal affairs are none of your business!"

Her cheeks bloomed with color, and she cast a stricken glance at Paul. "No pun intended!"

Vastly amused by this rare glimpse of his son being chastised by his wife, Paul chuckled. Peter winced. Patricia narrowed her eyes and gave her father-in-law a glittering look.

"Are you in love with some lucky lady?"

"Patricia!" Peter barked.

Giving up, Paul threw back his head and roared with laughter, unable to remember when he'd enjoyed the company of his family quite so thoroughly. If only Nicole and her husband were here, the day would be just about perfect, he thought as his laughter subsided. Just about, he corrected himself, envisioning the face that haunted his every waking hour.

"I'm sorry, Paul." Patricia's contrite tone drew Paul from his own thoughts. "I have no right—"

He cut her off gently. "Yes, you do. You have the right granted by affection and concern." Paul gazed at the son of his body and the daughter of his heart. Then he smiled. "I don't know if I'm in love. That's the reason I'm going home to pack. I must see her, talk to her." His mouth twisted into a wry smile. "She probably regards me as something of an old fool."

"You are not old!" Patricia protested indignantly.

"And far from a fool," Peter observed dryly. He studied Paul intently for a moment. Then an understanding, blatantly male grin revealed his hard white teeth. "Age hasn't a damn thing to do with it, Dad. *If* you love her."

Feeling oddly rejuvenated by their approval and support, Paul slid his chair back and stood up.

"That's what I intend to find out."

* * *

The traditional turkey-with-all-the-trimmings dinner was a smashing success. The disputed pumpkin pie was a smashing success. Karen was exhausted.

"Boy, I'm stuffed."

"That was the general idea." Karen smiled fondly at her youngest son. "First you stuff the bird, then you stuff yourself. It's the American way."

"Yeah." Mark's eyes glowed with happiness and contentment. "Thanksgiving's pretty neat."

"Yeah." Rand grinned. "It's almost as good as Christmas."

"Christmas!" Mark whooped. "Yeah! Will you still be here, Dad?"

"Yeah," Charles echoed enthusiastically.

"Yeah?" Karen chided, frowning.

"Aw, Mom, everybody says yeah," Rand grumbled.

"Yeah, they do." Mark nodded vigorously.

"And if everybody leaps off a cliff, will you follow?" Karen asked reasonably, her frown darkening as she noticed Charles's grinning encouragement of his sons. Annoyed, frustrated because it had always been this way, she shifted her frown to him. From the beginning Charles had opted to join forces with his sons, be one of the guys, while she'd been left with the role of disciplinarian.

"And you?" she charged. "Would you follow also?"

"Aw, Mom," Charles mimicked, earning laughter from his sons and indulgent smiles from his parents.

Karen couldn't win, and she knew it; besides, she was simply too darned tired to fight. Surrounded and outnumbered, Karen gave up the battle as gracefully as possible. Erasing her frown with a bright smile, she glanced at Judith and Randolf.

"Would you like coffee or tea or an after-dinner drink?"

"Coffee would be lovely." Judith smiled in appreciation of Karen's surrender. But then, as Karen knew well, Judith had always chosen to take the path of least resistance, which partially explained her son's lack of discipline.

"Coffee sounds good," Charles agreed.

"I think I'll have a brandy," Randolf said, sliding his chair away from the table.

"Why don't we have it in the living room?" Judith suggested, rising also. "It's so much more comfortable in there, and the fire's so cheery."

"Excellent idea, my dear." Randolf placed his hand at his wife's waist to escort her from the dining room. "Come along, Charles, we're in Karen's way here."

"Right." As Charles pushed back his chair, he arched his brows at Rand and Mark. "Why don't you guys go out into the fresh air. Go sink some baskets." He flicked his hand in the direction of the garage, indicating the rusting hoop with its tattered netting mounted on the side wall.

"Okay with me," Rand replied. He grinned challengingly at his brother. "Ill play you a game of one-on-one."

Mark scrambled off his chair. "You're on!"

Within a matter of seconds, Karen found herself standing alone in the dining room. A weary smile of acceptance twisted her lips as she gazed down at the remains of the holiday meal littering the two-hundred-year-old oval table.

What you need, Karen advised herself wryly, is a fairy godmother who isn't afraid of dipping her hands into hot dishwater. Or Judith's housekeeper, she revised as she began to stack her best china. If memory served, the housekeeper had been given the entire holiday weekend off.

Sighing softly, Karen turned to carry the first load of dishes into the kitchen, but paused at the sound of the front door slamming, followed by the aggrieved sound of Rand's voice.

"Hey, Dad! That basketball hoop's so loose it's about ready to fall off the wall. Can you fix it?"

"It's a holiday, Rand," Charles replied. "Make do today. I'll have your mother give the man who does the repairs a call tomorrow morning. Okay?"

"Yeah, I guess so." The door slammed again.

It's a holiday, Karen silently repeated, somewhat sarcastically. Damn, you could have fooled me! Telling herself to knock off the private pity party, she continued on into the kitchen. She didn't have time to wallow in self-pity; she had a table to clear, dishes, pots and a grease-spattered roast pan to clean, and coffee and brandy to serve. Boy! Aren't holidays fun!

By ten that night, Karen decided that there was a lot to be said for wallowing in self-pity; Charles was having tremendous success with the ploy. All he had to do was look dissatisfied and every member of the family leaped to make him comfortable.

She groaned with sheer bliss as she slipped into bed. Closing her eyes, Karen soaked in the blessed quiet.

Maybe, just maybe, she thought as she began to drift toward sleep, tomorrow will be less hectic.

It wasn't.

Karen was awakened early the following morning by two disgustingly wide-awake boys and their grinning father, all demanding to be fed. She was up and running from the moment her feet hit the floor.

The day was fine, crisp and cold. After breakfast, Randolf suggested an invigorating stroll on the beach. His suggestion was agreed to with enthusiasm. En masse, Judith, Randolf, Charles, Rand and Mark bundled up in warm jackets, gloves and assorted caps and scarves, then trooped merrily out the door.

Standing beside yet another cluttered table, Karen waved them on their way, grateful for the lull that enabled her to clean up the kitchen, make the beds and dump the first load of laundry into the washer in peace. It also afforded her a quiet minute in which to make the call to Gil Rawlins about fastening the basketball hoop; Gil was out of town for the weekend. Positive the boys, and Rand in particular, would be disappointed, Karen considered tackling the job herself, then rejected the idea. Who would get the meals and clean up afterward if she fell off the ladder and broke a bone?

No sooner had Karen finished in the kitchen than the red-cheeked, bright-eyed beach strollers trooped back into the house, requesting lunch. As she had surmised, the first words out of Rand's mouth were about the basketball hoop. To Karen's relief, though, he accepted her negative report with a philosophical shrug. At that moment, he was obviously more concerned with filling the emptiness inside his body than with exercise.

"Can I have a club sandwich made with the left-over turkey?" he asked.

"Oh, but—" Karen began, meaning to tell Rand that she was planning to use the leftover meat in a turkey pie for dinner. She never got the words out of her mouth.

"My, that does sound lovely," Judith agreed with her grandson. "I'll have the same."

Inwardly concluding that just about *everything* sounded lovely to Judith, Karen shrugged and decided broiled steaks would do as well for dinner. Lean steak was more in line with Charles's diet anyway.

Lunch was a pleasantly congenial meal. Karen thoroughly enjoyed the lively conversation once all the triple-decker sandwiches had been prepared and served. Between voracious bites of food, the boys regaled her with an in-depth account of all the shells they'd found on the beach and how much fun it had been having their grandparents as well as their father help collect them.

Though Karen found it nearly impossible to imagine the designer-attired Judith, Randolf and Charles grubbing in the sand for seashells, she smiled and took the boys' word for it, pleased the outing had been a success. There had been moments, too many in number, when Karen had suffered twinges of conscience and regret about denying her sons the fullness of a cohesive family experience. Gazing into the boys' animated faces, she decided the weekend was worth all the extra work and occasional irritation.

They were lingering over coffee and dessert when the front doorbell rang. Rand was already standing, since he had just asked to be excused from the table.

"I'll get it," he called, loping out of the dining room and down the hall.

"Now who could that be?" Judith wondered aloud.

"I haven't the vaguest idea." Karen shrugged.

"You weren't expecting more company, were you?" Charles asked, looking both suspicious and annoyed.

"No," Karen said, bristling at his proprietary attitude.

"Can I help you, sir?" they heard Rand ask in his best prep school manner.

Everyone grew quiet as they listened for a response. It came in a deep, attractive male voice that froze Karen's mind and shot adrenaline through her system.

"Yes. My name is Paul Vanzant. Is Ms. Mitchell in?"

Chapter Ten

The teenager had to be Rand.

Staring into the tall, skinny boy's brown eyes, Paul could see a masculine teenage image of Karen. He decided he liked the kid on sight.

"Hey, Mom, there's a man here who wants to see you."

Rand's voice broke in midsentence. Paul suppressed the urge to smile, recalling how embarrassed Peter had been at the same age when his voice had been changing. Then the urge to smile vanished, to be replaced by a humming tension as Karen, her face pale, her posture rigid, walked out of the dining alcove and along the hall toward him.

"You should have invited Mr. Vanzant inside, Rand, instead of keeping him standing outside in the cold."

Outside in the cold. Paul felt a bone-deep chill. He could sense her withdrawal. She was closing him out, had closed him out. Despair coiling in his mind, Paul stepped inside. After closing the door, Rand stood, his gaze moving from Paul to his mother. Karen didn't say a word; she didn't have to. The pointed look she leveled at her son said it all.

Rand shuffled his feet and cleared his throat. "Ah, I guess I'll, um, go talk to Dad," he stuttered, lowering his eyes.

"I think that's a good idea." Karen kept her gaze steady on Rand until he loped along the hall to the alcove.

Throughout the exchange, Paul felt the chill inside him intensify. A tremor of shock ripped through him when Rand mentioned his father. Charles was at the house! For the holiday or—? Ruthlessly cutting off the thought, Paul narrowed his eyes. Questions crowded his mind, but he held them at bay, waiting for Karen to make the first move. When she did, her voice was so strained that Paul was afraid he already knew the answers.

"Paul, what are you doing here. Why have you—"

"Here?" he interrupted her, sweeping the hallway with a glance. His remote tone and arched brows silenced her. She looked helpless for an instant. Then she sighed. Paul's own chest heaved in response.

"Come into the living room, please." Avoiding his stare, she turned to lead the way into the room Paul felt he knew more intimately than his bedroom at home. And yet her attitude made him feel like a stranger, an unwelcome stranger. The feeling induced a mixture of emotions in Paul, the strongest of which was anger.

"Won't you sit down?"

So polite, Paul thought, she's so damn polite. Suppressing an urge to grab her by the shoulders and shake her while demanding to know why she was shutting him out, Paul curled his fingers into his palms and decided he'd be damned if he'd play polite word games with her.

"Charles is here for the holiday?" he asked bluntly.

Karen flinched at his harsh tone but met his stare directly. "No." Her tone was even, inflectionless. "Charles has been here for over a month. I brought him back with me a week after he was released from the hospital." She drew a quick breath before continuing with her explanation. "Rand and Mark are home for the holiday, and Charles's parents are visiting. They picked the boys up at school and drove them home."

"I see." Paul smiled; it was either smile or curse. "Just one big happy family, hmm?"

Karen winced as though she'd been struck. "Paul, please—" She broke off and bit her lip.

"I'm sorry." Paul gave in to the need to swear softly under his breath. Self-disgust underlined each muttered syllable. He had lashed out in reaction to the fear creeping through him, and he had hurt her, insulted her. It was not like him, not at all like him, and yet . . .

Moving abruptly, he walked to the fireplace. He stared into the low, flickering flames, seeing in the blazing depths scenes of other, more satisfying moments spent in the room with her. His body tightening in response to memories as hot and vivid as the

crackling fire, Paul raised his head and turned to gaze
at her through eyes shielded by lowered eyelids. "I
never even considered the possibility that I might be
interrupting your holiday." His voice was low, reflecting the tightness gripping his body. "I never even
considered the probability of your boys being home."
A self-mocking smile briefly moved his lips. "All I
thought about was my need to see you, to talk to you."
He paused to examine her expression and eyes. Her
eyes were shadowed by a wounded look; her features
were pinched with lines of weariness.

Anger flared in Paul. When they had parted five
weeks ago, Karen's face had revealed both her inner
battle concerning her passionate, if brief, relationship with him and consternation over the possible effects of Charles's heart attack. Now, a mere five weeks
later, her eyes still betrayed inner conflict, but she appeared on the point of exhaustion.

What in the hell is he doing to her? The question
seared Paul's mind and strengthened his resolve.
Drawing a deep breath, he said, "I had planned on
staying awhile, to give us time to get to know each
other." He smiled faintly. "And to give myself time to
find out if what I suspect is true."

"What you suspect?" Karen repeated, shaking her
head. "Paul, I don't understand. What do you suspect?"

"That I'm falling in love with you."

For one perfect, brilliant instant, undiluted joy
shimmered through Karen. Paul was here, near
enough to touch. Her fingers itched with the need to
reach out and seek proof of his reality. Her lips burned

with a fire only his mouth could quench. Her empty body ached for a completion he alone could give. Within that perfect instant, Karen could envision an end to endless nights of longing. Paul was here. She was whole. Life was radiant.

And then the instant ended.

Reality waited in the dining alcove. And reality was unchanged by a man who suspected that he was falling in love.

The death of the perfect instant left the agony of an imperfect reality. How many times since the day she had driven away, leaving him calling after her, had she secretly, silently cried out for him? How many times in all the long nights since then had she awakened, her body quivering with the need to be a part of his? Karen shivered in response to the answers that washed through her mind.

And now Paul was here, offering her the possibility of a different, brighter reality. But she could not let him stay. Karen had not sought love, had not wanted to love ever again. But she did love, was in love. She didn't suspect it; she was certain of it. And she could not let him stay.

The realization that she must deny herself and send Paul away struck Karen like a blow. She swayed with the shattering backlash.

"Karen!" His tone sharp with alarm, Paul stepped toward her.

Karen stepped back. Drawing in deep, controlling breaths, she held up a hand as if to ward him off.

"I'm all right." Her reedy voice belied her assurances. Straightening her spine, tightening her body and her nerves, Karen steeled herself to say what had to be said. The words of rejection and dismissal never made it from her mind to her lips.

"Aren't you going to introduce us to your guest, Karen?"

Karen jolted at the sound of speculation woven through the pleasant tone of Charles's voice. Reality was here and now, in the form of Charles and his parents sauntering into the room and the infinitely more important forms of the two wary-eyed boys hovering in the doorway.

Acceptance was not unlike the feel of living death. For a millisecond, rebellion flared inside Karen; then, just as quickly, it was extinguished.

"Yes, of course." Karen was amazed at the even, casual sound of her voice. She was more amazed at her ability to smile as she turned to face them. "Charles, Judith, Randolf, this is Mr. Vanzant." She shifted to look at Paul without looking at him at all. "Mr. Vanzant, I'd like you to meet Charles Mitchell." She indicated the man who had come to stand beside her. "And his parents, Judith and Randolf Mitchell." Her smile grew easier as she glanced at the doorway. "And the boys are Rand and Mark."

Paul responded to the disruptive interruption like the gentleman and aristocrat he was. His expression cool but polite, he extended his hand as he moved forward. "Charles." Paul gripped Charles's hand briefly, then released it and turned to his parents. "Mr. Mitchell. Mrs. Mitchell."

"Mr. Vanzant." The three Mitchells responded in unison.

"Paul, please," he murmured vaguely, gazing at the two boys in the doorway. A faint smile relieved the coolness of his expression and lit his dark eyes from within. "Rand?" Paul stared at the older boy. At Rand's nod, he shifted his gaze. "Mark." With three long strides, Paul was across the room, extending his hand with the same respect he had afforded the adults. "I'm pleased to meet you both."

Wide-eyed and obviously surprised at receiving the same consideration as their elders, Rand and Mark hesitantly extended their own, smaller hands. The grip was completed, establishing contact on various levels of awareness. Both youngsters revealed pleasurable confusion.

A bittersweet ache filled Karen as she watched the man she loved touch her sons, physically and emotionally. The ache expanded as she watched each boy's reluctant response. The thought of what might have been teased the edges of her mind. With ruthless determination, Karen shoved the thought aside. The situation was growing more impossible by the minute. The glint of speculation in Charles's eyes was solidifying into . . . what?

"Vanzant." Randolf murmured the name in bemused contemplation.

Karen blinked and glanced at Randolf. As she looked at him, he frowned and murmured the name again.

"Vanzant?" This time his murmur held a questioning note.

Mentally shrugging off Randolf's odd behavior, Karen switched her gaze to the man turning to face her. Paul's stare was compelling; she couldn't maintain it and speak the words of dismissal. Her gaze shifted to Charles. "Mr. Vanzant was just—"

"Speaking to that colorful character who runs the store in town," Paul finished for her. "He told me that even though the bed-and-breakfast was closed for the season, Ms. Mitchell might be willing to accommodate me."

Karen was consumed by equal measures of elation and despair. She knew he couldn't stay but, but ... Hope leaped higher than the flames in the fireplace.

"You want to rent a room?" Charles exclaimed. "Here?"

"Yes."

"But—"

"Paul Vanzant." No longer a murmur, Randolf's contemplative tone cut through his son's protest and drew a varied response from his audience.

Both Karen and Judith frowned in confusion.

Charles scowled impatiently.

Paul arched his brows in mild inquiry.

"The Philadelphia banker Vanzant?" Randolf asked, ignoring his family as he centered his attention on Paul.

"Yes." Smiling wryly, Paul inclined his head. And unbeknownst to Karen, with his quiet confirmation, choice and decision were plucked from her hands.

Randolf took command of the situation. Smiling broadly, he again extended his hand to grasp Paul's. "I've wanted to meet you for years but somehow kept missing the opportunity. It really is a pleasure to meet you, sir." The term of respect from the older man said reams more than his actual words. "And I'm positive Karen will be delighted to accommodate you." He beamed at Karen. "Won't you, my dear?"

What could she say? Karen hesitated as her options skipped through her mind. Then she granted Randolf's request—simply because she wanted to. "Yes, if you insist." She was careful not to look at Paul or Charles.

"Well, of course I insist." A flicker of a frown crossed his face as he noted his son's scowl. "Charles, Judith." Reaching out, he drew his wife to his side. "Surely you both remember all the times I've mentioned Mr. Vanzant's name?" Randolf glanced from one to the other. Impatience flashed in his eyes as he encountered a blank stare from Charles and a vague smile from Judith. "Good heavens!" he exploded. "How could either one of you forget the name of the banker who saved our company from financial ruin?" he demanded, conveniently forgetting that he himself had spent several minutes capturing the memory.

"It was a long time ago, Mr. Mitchell," Paul inserted in an attempt to ease the tension.

"Randolf, please," he murmured in an echo of Paul's earlier request. "But you're correct, of course. It was a long time ago." Randolf smiled at his son. "Charles was still in college." He looked pensive. "He very probably wouldn't have graduated if it hadn't been for you, Paul," he admitted with simple honesty.

Judith gasped in surprise. Charles bristled visibly.

"Dad, really, I'm sure it wasn't as bad as all that!"

"Are you indeed?" Randolf's head snapped up, revealing the shrewd businessman he'd become in the years between his son's college days and Charles's current position as vice president of the firm under discussion. "Then you'd better reorganize your thinking. I was within a hairsbreadth of losing everything.'' His features grew taut with remembrance. ''And I mean literally everything. I had unwisely extended myself. I had been refused help by every banker in Boston and several other cities.'' His expression eased as he glanced at Paul. ''Paul was the only one with the guts to back me. And he did it sight unseen, through my representative.'' A flush of color tinged his cheeks. ''I never thanked you personally.''

Paul's smile was easy and meltingly attractive. ''You thanked me many times over by confirming the faith I had in your ideas for company expansion and your ability to make them work.''

Fascinated by the conversation and the insight it gave her into a previously unsuspected facet of Paul's character, Karen was unconscious of the fact that Paul was still wearing his jacket, that they were all standing in the center of the living room and that the boys had disappeared at some point or other during the discussion. Paul, on the other hand, was obviously aware of everything that went on around him.

''I wonder if I might remove my jacket?'' Though his expression and tone were scrupulously polite, the eyes he directed to Karen had a familiar devilish gleam. ''It's quite warm in here.''

''Oh!'' Karen flushed with embarrassment.

''Good grief!'' Randolf muttered.

''How terribly rude of us all!'' Judith fluttered.

Charles remained silent, staring resentfully at the cause of the sudden confusion and the reason for a revelation he obviously hadn't enjoyed. But then, he didn't need to say anything; his disapproval of Paul was a palpable force in the atmosphere.

Sparing a frown for Charles, Karen walked to Paul, hand outstretched. "I am sorry, Mr. Vanzant. Please do take off your jacket."

"Paul, I insist." The devilish gleam brightened in his eyes as Paul shrugged out of the garment. Ignoring Charles and his flustered parents for an instant, he smiled for Karen alone. "Thank you." His murmured response encompassed much more than appreciation of being relieved of the heavy outdoor coat.

"You're welcome." Karen's reply encompassed much more than an automatic social response. For the length of a sighing breath, their gazes tangled, meshed, blended.

"Have you had lunch, Paul?" Randolf's inquiring tone revealed his lack of awareness of the dreamlike spell cocooning Karen and Paul. At the same time, his voice shattered the moment.

Paul's lips twisted as he reluctantly glanced away from the soft glow in Karen's eyes. "As a matter of fact, I completely forgot about lunch." His shoulders lifted in a half shrug. "I quite often do."

"Well, we'll take care of that," Randolf returned heartily. "Won't we, Karen?" But before she could respond, he added, "Karen makes the most fantastic turkey club sandwiches."

On her way to the closet in the hallway, Karen paused in the doorway, her fingers digging into the down-filled jacket. Randolf's reference to sandwiches reminded her of the lunch debris waiting for her on the alcove table. Resigning herself to kitchen duty, she was about to offer Paul something when Randolf spoke again.

"Was there any meat left, Karen?"

As she turned, Karen worked her lips into a smile. "Yes, plenty. Would you like a sandwich and a cup of coffee, Paul?"

"No sandwich, really." Paul smiled at her. "But I would appreciate the coffee."

"And we'll all have a cup with you, keep you company," Randolf said expansively. "How about a piece of pumpkin pie with it? Karen made it, and it's delicious."

"I'm sure it is, but no thank you." Paul glanced at Karen and smiled apologetically. "I'm sorry, but I never really liked pumpkin pie."

It was ridiculous, Karen chided herself. It was childish and silly. And yet she couldn't control the rush of pleasure his admission gave her or the satisfying sense of sharing a link with him, even such a ridiculous, tenuous link.

"That's all right, I—" She started to tell him she also never really liked the dessert, but once again, Randolf hastened to enlighten the other man.

"No need to apologize, Paul. It seems you and Karen have something in common." He chuckled as Paul sliced a glance at him and arched a questioning eyebrow. "She doesn't like it, either."

"Really?" His tone inflectionless, his expression bland, Paul returned his gaze to Karen; she alone saw the warmth flickering in his dark eyes.

"There were croissants left over at breakfast," she said in her best hostess tones, thrilling to the light that flared in the dark depths of his eyes. "I'd be happy to warm some in the microwave for you if you'd like."

"Yes, thank you." His heated gaze caressed her. "I'd like that very much."

Another link had been forged between them; Karen knew it, but more importantly, she was suddenly aware that Paul realized it, too. Energy flowed through her, sweeping her weariness away. Her step light, she walked from the room, calling over her shoulder, "Make yourselves comfortable. I'll only be a minute."

As had happened after all the previous meals they'd shared, not one of the Mitchells offered assistance. Karen didn't care. Paul was there, back in her house, back in her living room, back in her life. Humming to herself, she made child's play out of the cleaning-up routine and had completed most of it before the coffee was finished.

After serving the coffee and croissants, Karen sat quietly, offering little to the conversation, content to simply be close to Paul once again.

He looked wonderful, she decided, studying him as she sipped the coffee she really didn't want. But there was a subtle change in Paul's appearance that puzzled her. Observing him, listening to him speak, Karen pondered the change, and then the answer struck her. The difference in Paul was not only in appearance but in attitude, as well. For all his aristocratic look, the man she'd first met on the beach had had an uncentered, rudderless look about him. The Paul now seated a few feet from her appeared purposeful and confident, the image of a man in control of his own life.

On reflection, it was obvious to Karen that something had occurred to transform Paul during the weeks they'd been separated. And with the memory of his near-confession of love for her singing in her mind,

Karen's pulse leaped with the thought that she was in part responsible for the change in him.

Karen was almost giddy with the possibilities that sprang from her speculative thought and was oblivious to the watchful, scowling expression on Charles's face. Paul, on the other hand, was very much aware of her former husband's discontent.

He's suspicious as hell and jealous because of it.
Even as the thought formed in his mind, Paul silently responded to it. The response was as hard as it was swift.
The hell with Mitchell.
His attention divided between the elder and the younger Mitchell men, Paul was nevertheless aware of Karen's soft gaze and her thorough scrutiny of him. More than anything else in the world, he wanted to be alone with her. While engaging in genial conversation with Randolf, his body tingled with anticipation. While he took Charles's measure, his nerves twanged with impatience. In fact, Paul required every ounce of willpower he possessed to keep himself from insulting the Mitchells by grabbing Karen and rudely walking from the room.

A silent sigh of relief shuddered through him when, at Randolf's suggestion, Karen rose to show Paul to his room. Keeping a respectful distance between them, he followed her from the room and up the stairs. A frown drew his eyebrows together when, at the landing at the top of the staircase, she turned toward the front of the house.

"You're giving me a different room?"
"Yes."

Paul's frown deepened at the evidence of strain in her voice. Assuming she was putting him in a room farther away from hers for appearance' sake, he chided gently, "But I liked the room I had before." He felt a premonitory flash of anger at the way her lips tightened before she replied.

"I can't give you that room, Paul. Charles is using it."

And is Charles using you, too? Paul clenched his teeth to keep from snarling the thought aloud. "I see," he murmured tightly, his anger mingling with fear as he stepped into the unfamiliar bedroom. Charles had been alone with Karen in the house for several weeks. Had he used those weeks to— Paul ruthlessly cut off the thought, actually afraid to follow it to its natural conclusion. The feeling he had experienced earlier of again being outside in the cold returned. Suddenly Paul had to know exactly where he stood with her. Moving decisively, he shut the door, enclosing them in privacy. Denying himself the right to touch her, he held her still by locking his gaze with hers.

"Has there been a reconciliation between you and Charles?"

"No!" Karen denied with a swiftness that was sweetly satisfying to Paul. "Charles is here to recuperate, and that is absolutely all he is here for."

"Then you don't want me to leave?" Paul asked, and held his breath.

"Leave!" Karen's anxious expression sent a shiver of relief through him. "No, Paul, I don't want you to leave."

"I'm delighted to hear you say that—" Paul flashed a rakish grin, "—since I had no intentions of leaving anyway."

Randolf monopolized practically every one of Paul's waking minutes throughout what was left of the weekend, so Karen saw very little of her unexpected tenant. And as Judith was forever at Randolf's side, Karen saw too much of Charles for her own peace of mind. Charles had taken to acting very strangely—at least whenever his parents weren't around.

Then, in addition to her resentment at being denied Paul's company and her annoyed concern over Charles's suddenly blatant show of affection for her—usually at mealtimes, when everybody was in attendance—Karen was puzzled by several seemingly unrelated incidents.

The first was not unexpected and occurred at the breakfast table the morning after Paul's arrival. Looking bored, Rand wolfed down his meal and asked to be excused from the table. He then prowled noisily from one room to another until Judith, frowning with concern, asked him what was troubling him, thereby giving him the opening he had obviously been waiting for.

"There's nothing to do," Rand complained in the grating tone of voice only children can achieve.

Charles dismissed Rand with a flick of his hand. "Go look for shells on the beach."

Karen shot a narrowed look at Charles. She had wondered how long his role of "buddy-father" would last. Karen had never doubted Charles's love for his sons, but she never overestimated his patience with them, either. It had always been thus; Charles could only take children in small doses, even his own children.

"We did that yesterday," Mark whined, jumping in to support his brother.

"For God's sake!" Charles threw his napkin on the table. "There's got to be something that you kids can do to amuse yourselves. Go shoot some baskets."

"Charles, you must not get upset!" Judith cautioned him in a soothing tone.

"How can I not get upset with all the aggravation in this place lately?" he demanded, sweeping his gaze from Rand to Mark and then to Paul.

Staring at his father, Rand's expression betrayed conflicting emotions of remorse and rebellion. Mark began to cry.

"We can't shoot baskets," he sniffled. "The hoop's ready to fall down."

"Well, find something to do," Charles ordered. "And I want you both to stop your damn complaining."

"Charles!" Judith exclaimed.

"Really, son," Randolf chastised.

"Don't swear at the boys." Karen's voice was low but contained a warning edge of steel, and her eyes were cold with purpose. "I mean it, Charles. As long as you're in my house, you will not curse at the boys. I won't tolerate it."

An angry, embarrassed flush climbed from Charles's neck to his cheeks.

"Oh, Karen, I'm sure he didn't mean it the way it sounded!" Judith protested her son's innocence.

"Of course he didn't!" Randolf insisted. "It was common language usage; a slip of the tongue."

"Yes. Common." As she turned to look at the elder Mitchells, Karen's gaze was snagged by watchful dark eyes. Paul hadn't said a word; words were unnecessary. The approval shining from his eyes championed her position. Feeling the strength of two, she faced her former in-laws. "The term is common, and I will not permit it to be used on my sons. Not even by their father." Without a blink, she swung her gaze to Rand and Mark. "If you are bored, you could always occupy yourselves by cleaning up your rooms."

"Aw, Mom!" Making a sour face, Rand stomped from the room. Looking at Karen as if he suspected she'd slipped a cog, Mark trailed after his brother.

"You're not letting them grow up," Charles sniped peevishly, slumping in his chair. "I'd bet they hear a lot worse than 'damn' from the other kids at school."

"I'm sure you're right." Pushing her chair back, Karen rose and began clearing the table. "But they are not going to hear it at home." Juggling the stacked dishes, she walked from the alcove.

As if her action had been a signal, the room emptied quickly. His expression much the same as Mark's when he was pouting, Charles picked up the morning paper and disappeared into the living room. After a murmured discussion, Judith and Randolf announced they were driving into town, then beat a hasty retreat. A smile curving his lips, Paul finished clearing the table.

"You don't have to do that." Not looking at him, afraid to trust herself to even glance at him, Karen methodically stacked the dishes in the dishwasher.

"I know." Just as methodically Paul rinsed the dishcloth and returned to the alcove to wipe the table.

Completing the loading quickly, Karen switched on the machine. "All done," she called to him, escaping into the laundry room. Even over the sound of water running into the kitchen sink as Paul again rinsed the cloth, Karen could hear his soft laughter.

The second incident occurred late in the morning and was really not so much an incident as a set of circumstances that induced an odd sense of confusion in Karen.

She was dusting the living room. The house had been unusually quiet for some time except for Charles, who had been underfoot all morning, making a supreme effort to be ingratiating and charming and getting very little response from Karen.

She was busy, and long since immune to his practiced lines. She was also distracted, which Charles didn't appreciate at all.

Where was everybody?

The question had been nagging at Karen intermittently for over an hour. Paul had vanished from the house before she'd emerged from the laundry room. She hadn't seen hide or hair of either of the boys since they'd stormed from the dining alcove. And, though Judith and Randolf had returned to the house after spending less than an hour in town, they had immediately gone out again, informing Karen that they were going to take a stroll on the beach.

Frowning at her own contrariness for fretting over the quiet after longing for quiet, Karen impatiently pulled her arm free when Charles caught her by the wrist.

"Why don't you leave that till later and sit down and talk to me?" he demanded, every bit as petulant as his thirteen-year-old son when he was down with a cold.

"It has to be done, Charles." Karen repeated the phrase she'd uttered countless times during the weeks he'd been there, wondering, as usual, how he thought the work got done if she didn't do it.

"Can't it wait?"

"For whom?"

Charles subsided with a disgruntled sigh. Smiling wryly, Karen continued dusting. She was arranging a copper potpourri pot on a gleaming, newly dusted table when all the missing persons appeared at once, shattering the quiet.

Judith and Randolf were in fine spirits and ready for lunch, which didn't surprise or confuse Karen.

Paul was quiet but not exceptionally so, which didn't surprise or confuse her, either.

It was Rand's and Mark's attitude that gave her an odd sense of confusion. Their eyes were bright, their cheeks glowed with healthy color from the sting of the cold sea breeze, and not a trace of their earlier pouty moodiness remained in either young face. Saying little, they both consumed their lunch at their usual starving-animal speed. The instant they had drained the last drop of milk from their glasses, Rand and Mark politely asked to be excused from the table. Seconds later, the front door banged shut.

Were they coming down with something? Karen asked herself. They had behaved too well, been too quiet. They hadn't even exchanged one insult, let alone their regulation number!

The third incident was comprised entirely of a familiar sound that registered on Karen later that afternoon.

The house had grown quiet again after lunch, but this time Karen knew, or at least had an idea, where everyone was. The boys had not returned after leaving the lunch table; Karen assumed they were scavenging for shells on the beach. Judith was ensconced in a chair in the living room, lost to the world in a murder mystery she'd picked up in town. Randolf had taken Paul off somewhere to talk business. Charles, irritated and frustrated by Karen's refusal to take anything he said seriously, had gone to his room for a nap. And Karen, realizing she had caught up with the daily chores, had decided to wallow in a long, hot bath.

Her skin rosy from the hot water and softened from the oil beads she'd tossed into it, Karen took her time dressing. Telling herself it had absolutely nothing to do with a desire to appear attractive to Paul, she very carefully applied just a tad more makeup than usual.

Thinking of Paul, remembering him in her room, in her bed, sent icy chills down her spine and warmth to her face. Light-headed with memories and a rush of emotions too numerous to sort out before starting dinner, Karen was already in a pleasant state of confusion as she drifted out of her room.

She heard the sound vaguely as she entered the kitchen but, caught up in an echoing memory of a man telling her he thought he was falling in love, Karen took no notice of it. It was after she had gently come back to earth to face the necessity of preparing a meal for seven hungry people that the sound intruded on her consciousness.

It was the steady thump-thump of a basketball being bounced on a macadam surface and then the solid twang of the ball striking a firmly attached hoop before dropping through a basket.

Chapter Eleven

By itself, the solid sound of a basketball striking the rim of a well-anchored hoop would not have been cause for in-depth consideration for Karen, had it not been for the fact that the looseness of that very hoop had precipitated the scene at breakfast.

Obviously someone had tightened the hoop—but who? Karen frowned in consternation.

Paul. His name leaped into her mind as if it belonged there.

Ridiculous! Karen shook her head, negating the very idea. Aside from the fact that Paul had made the repairs necessary to prepare the house for the coming winter, he had been walking and talking very softly since his arrival the day before, and she couldn't think of a single reason why Paul would feel inclined to accommodate two fractious teenage boys.

Since Karen was equally certain Charles hadn't attempted the job or even thought of doing so, that left Randolf. Yet she found it nearly impossible to imagine her very proper sixty-four-year-old former father-in-law dragging out the necessary tools, then teetering precariously on a ladder, even for his grandsons.

Of course, there was always the possibility that, impatient with the situation, Rand and Mark had decided to take matters into their own hands and fasten the hoop themselves. Possible but improbable. Karen knew her sons. Rand and Mark were both quick and agile when it came to participation in almost any sport. But the other side of their personality coin revealed an almost total lack of coordination in any and all activities that were domestic in origin. In other words, both boys were all thumbs around the house.

Karen readily accepted the responsibility for Rand's and Mark's ineptitude, and she found it hard to believe they had attacked the chore of fixing the hoop, no matter how restless and bored they were. But if not the boys, then who had accomplished the task?

Feeling as though her mind had completed a fruitless circle, Karen shrugged her shoulders. Speculation was getting her nowhere, and she had a meal to prepare. Besides, all she had to do to solve the mystery was raise the question at the dinner table.

Karen broached the subject the minute they were all seated and served. "Did I hear you guys shooting baskets a little while ago?" she asked casually.

"Uh-huh," Rand murmured around the food in his mouth.

"But I thought you couldn't shoot because the hoop was too lose."

Mark grinned happily. "It's fixed now.

"That's nice." Karen held on to her patience, reminding herself that children were only forthcoming when you didn't want them to be. "Who fixed it?"

"Mr. Vanzant." Rand supplied the answer between swallowing and shoveling another forkful of mashed potatoes into his mouth.

"Yeah," Mark concurred. "Mr. Vanzant fixed it right after we got back from our walk on the beach."

Concerned with filling the emptiness in their respective stomachs, neither boy noticed as four pairs of adult eyes homed in on Paul Vanzant. Nor did they note the adult facial expressions displayed, ranging from resentment in their father's face to amazement on the faces of their mother and grandparents to wry amusement on the face of the man the others were staring at.

"You tightened the hoop, Paul?" Randolf asked, sliding a glance over Paul's hand-tailored slacks and cashmere sweater, then to his well-cared-for hands.

"Guilty as charged," Paul confessed.

"Why?" Charles's voice was grating.

Paul slowly turned to give Charles his undivided attention. "Why not?" he countered reasonably.

"It wasn't necessary." Charles glared at Paul. "The handyman would have fixed it Monday."

"To what purpose?" Paul asked reasonably. "The boys won't be here on Monday."

Nonplussed and obviously frustrated, Charles pushed his chair away from the table and stood up. "This discussion is ridiculous!" His lips twisting unpleasantly, he stared at Karen. "All this fuss because two kids can't amuse themselves for one afternoon."

Though he didn't add, "And it's all your fault," the accusation was implicit in his tone.

"Charles, please, calm yourself." Judith moved to get up. "This upheaval isn't good for you!"

"I know." He sighed heavily. "I don't feel too well. I think I'll lie down for a while." Without waiting for a reaction, he strode from the room.

Murmuring "Oh, dear!" Judith rushed after him. Jumping up, Randolf was right behind her.

For long seconds, silence weighted the room. Paul broke it gently. "I'm sorry. I certainly didn't mean—"

Karen interrupted him. "It's not your fault."

"No, it's my fault." Rand's cheeks were pale.

Karen's tone became brisk. "No, Rand, it isn't. There was no reason for your father to get worked up over this." Her shoulders moved in a helpless shrug. "I don't know why he was so upset, but then, I never did understand his sudden mood swings."

"Is Daddy okay, Mom?" Mark asked, blinking to stem the tears filling his eyes.

Furious with Charles and silently condemning him for frightening his sons, Karen got up and circled the table. Standing between Rand and Mark, she hugged their trembling bodies close to her own. "I'm sure your dad is fine," she murmured soothingly.

"But, what if—" Rand's voice failed, and he stared up at her fearfully. Before Karen could form words of reassurance, Paul responded to the question Rand could not force himself to ask.

"If your father isn't okay, we'll drive him into Portland to see a doctor."

Rand turned to Paul. His hopeful yet fearful expression caused a wrenching pain in Karen's chest. "You will, Mr. Vanzant? I mean, you will be here with Mom, drive Dad to see a doctor?"

Paul's serious expression was eased by a gentle, understanding smile. "Yes, Rand. I promise you I will be here."

Karen was caught between the urge to smile and the need to sigh. She also understood exactly what kind of reassurance Rand was seeking. Hovering on the edge of manhood, Rand needed to know that there would be another man in the house to take control if Charles suffered another attack.

And she had actually believed she'd instilled in her sons the concept of equality between the sexes. Karen gave in to the sigh.

With one child seeming satisfied, the other had to be heard from. His lower lip trembling, Mark gazed pleadingly at Karen. "Do we have to go back to school tomorrow, Mom?"

"Yes." Karen's tone was clear, with a no-arguments firmness.

"But what if...something happens?" A fresh surge of tears spilled onto Mark's cheeks.

"Then I'll come and get you and bring you home." Paul again answered for Karen. Then he made a suggestion that normally would have elicited surprised protests from Rand and Mark. "But for right now, if you want to feel useful, you could help your mother by clearing the table."

Karen was amazed, not only by his suggestion but by her admittedly pampered sons' reaction to it. They nearly knocked her over in their haste to do his bidding.

Telling herself she should feel angry or at least impatient with Paul for arrogantly taking control from her, Karen could not deny the feeling of relief that swept through her. In his steady, dependable tone of voice, Paul had relieved Rand's and Mark's anxiety and, to a great extent, her own. Karen felt weak with gratitude. At the same time, she felt a sharp twinge of curiosity. It was obvious from their acceptance of his words that both boys believed Paul and trusted him to make good on his promises. How, she wondered, had Paul managed to gain their trust in such a short period of time?

Pondering the question, Karen moved to help with the cleaning up but went still as she remembered Mark telling them that Paul had fixed the basketball hoop after their walk on the beach. But was one walk on the beach enough to instill trust? she asked herself. An answer sprang into her mind immediately. Hadn't she reacted with the same feeling of trust in Paul after a brief meeting on the beach? A frown tugging her eyebrows together, Karen raised her head to stare at him.

"Something wrong?" Paul asked, his eyes darkening with concern.

"No, not wrong." Karen shook her head. "I'm just curious about what you and the kids talked about during your stroll on the beach."

A light of understanding and amusement relieved the darkness shadowing his eyes; a smile eased the tense lines around his mouth. "Heavy stuff," he murmured, slanting a quick glance toward the kitchen to make sure the boys were beyond the reach of his low-pitched voice. "Life and sex and the difficulty of making the big step between the security of adolescence and the responsibility of manhood."

The traditional father-son discussion! Karen was struck speechless at the very idea. How many times had she asked Charles to initiate such a discussion with his sons? Karen didn't have to search for an answer; she had first made the request of Charles when Rand had celebrated his thirteenth birthday more than two years ago. In his familiar, unconcerned way, Charles had laughed, called her old-fashioned and insisted the boys could very probably instruct him on the subject. Of course, it had been a cop-out for Charles. Karen hadn't been in the least surprised; Charles had been copping out on everything serious all his adult life. But Paul was very obviously cut from much stronger cloth, Karen concluded—and not for the first time.

"You don't approve?"

Realizing that she was probably scowling, Karen smiled at him. "It isn't that I don't approve." She lifted her shoulders in a slight shrug. "I'm just surprised that you'd bother, that's all."

"Bother?" Paul repeated, giving her an odd look. "It wasn't a bother. I enjoyed our conversation." His smile was soft with reminiscence. "It's been a long time since I engaged in that type of basic discussion." He laughed. "Besides, it exercised my mind. Those kids of yours are very bright. They tossed some tough questions at me."

Parental pride flowed through Karen, warming her and easing the tension left over from the scene Charles had created. "They have their difficult moments but—" she smiled hesitantly as she raised her eyes to his "—they're pretty good kids, aren't they?" Karen wasn't quite sure why his opinion was so important to her; she only knew it was.

Paul's answering smile glowed in his eyes before it reached his lips. "They are very good kids, Karen. You have every right to be proud of them." His lips curved with heart-touching tenderness as he lifted his hand to her face.

"Mom?" Rand's call halted Paul's fingers an inch from her cheek, and with a philosophical smile, he drew his hand away.

"Yes?" Karen responded, strangely breathless.

"The dishwasher's loaded and running and everything's cleaned up. Can me and Mark watch TV now?"

Karen corrected his grammar automatically. "Can Mark and I."

"Aw, Mom!" Rand's groan blended with Paul's low chuckle. "Can we?"

Without conscious thought, Karen looked at Paul with a silent plea for his opinion of the request. A flicker of surprise moved across his face and briefly widened his eyes, quickly followed by an expression of deep pleasure. Holding her gaze with his, he slowly nodded his head. Again without thought, Karen acted on his judgment.

"Yes, you may," she called, laughing as the boys took off like a shot, as if afraid she'd change her mind if they didn't disappear from her sight immediately.

Paul went still, his expression expectant; then he grinned. "Isn't the silence wonderful?" he asked in a stage whisper.

"Beautiful," Karen breathed on a sigh.

"Let's escape." Paul's eyes gleamed with playfulness, and his grin broadened.

He looked so much like a little boy up to mischief that Karen burst out laughing. "Escape!" she gasped. "To where?"

"The beach?" One dark eyebrow arched rakishly.

"But it's freezing outside!"

The slanting glance he gave her had more the look of the devil than any little boy Karen had ever known. "Yes, but consider the fun we could have keeping each other warm."

Fun! Try as she might, Karen couldn't remember the last time she'd done something just for the fun of it. And if she was honest with herself, she had to admit that his suggestion had appeal, a lot of appeal. Yet she hesitated, telling herself she really shouldn't leave the house. The boys might need her for something. She had guests. Charles was obviously not feeling well. No, she really shouldn't leave the house. But...Karen looked into Paul's eyes and was lost.

"I'd love a breath of fresh air."

The words were barely out of her mouth before Paul grasped her hand and took off down the hall to the closet. Cautioning her to be quiet by placing one finger across his lips, he carefully removed their jackets. After helping her with hers, he urged her toward the back door, pulling his jacket on as he walked. A loud sigh of relief whooshed through his lips as he shut the door behind them.

"Ah, alone at last," he said teasingly, reaching for her hand. "I was beginning to think I'd have to kidnap you to have a private conversation."

Laughing spontaneously, Karen slid her hand into his and felt a thrill as he entwined her fingers in his. "Where would you kidnap me to?" she asked, feeling suddenly lighthearted and young again. "I hope someplace decadent and exotic," she added before he could respond.

"Decadent and exotic, hmm?" Paul murmured. He drew her with him as he stepped off the veranda. "I'll have to think about that." His expression somber, contemplative, he strolled onto the beach.

Though cold, the night was still. Instead of their more usual thundering rush to crash into the beach, the ocean waves swelled gently before caressing the shore with a murmured swish. "Take your time," Karen said, tilting her head back to gaze up at the brilliance of millions of stars and one incredibly beautiful pale yellow moon. "What a gorgeous night!" she whispered in an awed tone. "Just look at that sky."

Lifting his head, Paul stared at the heavens a moment before transferring his gaze to her face. "I'd rather look at you." Untwining their fingers, he released her hand to bring his arm up and around her shoulders, drawing her body close to the warmth of his. Lowering his head, Paul brushed his lips over her ear. "You're beautiful, Karen," he murmured. "And much more inspiring to me than the light of trillions of stars."

Excitement charged through Karen, stealing her breath, clouding her senses. Need nipped at the heels of excitement, the need to hold him, touch him, taste him. Her lips parted with eager anticipation as he drew his mouth in a tantalizing line to hers.

"Oh, Paul." Her voice was a whisper that misted his lips.

"Say it again." With maddening slowness, he brushed his lips back and forth over hers. "I want to hear you say my name again."

"Paul."

"Lord, Karen, I missed you unbearably." Raising his other arm, he crushed her willing body to his. "I thought I'd go crazy with wanting you while we were apart," he groaned, taking her mouth fiercely.

His kiss was hard, impatient, fiery and wonderful. Curling her arms around his neck, Karen clung to him, taking everything from him, giving everything to him. Had she actually convinced herself she could continue to exist without ever again experiencing the spiraling heat and excitement only Paul could generate inside her? she asked herself muzzily, stroking his teasing tongue with her own. The mere thought of never again knowing the safety of his embrace, feeling the power of his kiss, sent a wave of cold fear through her, and her mouth became desperate with hunger.

Paul's hands moved restlessly over Karen's bulky jacket, searching for the soft woman beneath the heavy material. He muttered a curse as he drew his lips from hers to explore her face. "I want to undress you," he murmured, skimming his lips over her closed eyelids. "I need to feel you, all of you, against me."

"Yes," Karen sighed. Then reality intruded. "Paul, we can't!" she cried.

"I know." His breath shuddered from his body as he rested his forehead against hers. "I know."

They stood clasping one another, silently comforting each other until the cold penetrated their jackets to chill their bodies. Paul dropped his arms and stepped back when Karen shivered involuntarily.

"You're freezing," he said, moving away from her. "I must take you inside."

Although Karen knew he was right, she held out against reason. "But we didn't have our conversation."

"No?" Paul asked with wry amusement. "I thought we said a great deal." Taking her hand in his, he started for the house. They were almost to the veranda steps before he spoke again. "Randolf tells me that he and Judith are driving the kids back to school tomorrow."

"Yes. Then they'll go on to Boston." Karen glanced at him. "Why?"

Paul answered with a question. "Charles will be staying here?"

Karen lowered her gaze to the veranda steps. "Yes. At least until after the Christmas holidays."

"Then so will I." Paul's voice was soft, but steely with determination.

"You knew him before, didn't you?"

Monday mornings had never been Karen's best times and being interrogated by a moody ex-husband on a Monday morning following a tiring holiday was the absolute pits. Gritting her teeth, Karen slowly turned away from the coffee maker to face Charles.

His expression stormy, his lips flattened into a thin line of disapproval, Charles glared at her from the doorway.

"Him?" Karen asked, being deliberately obtuse.

"Vanzant." Not unlike a toddler in a fit of temper, Charles stomped to the table and dropped onto a chair. "You knew him before he arrived here Friday afternoon, didn't you?"

Karen considered denial or evasion for a moment but decided it wasn't worth the effort. "Yes, I met Paul over a month ago," she replied quietly.

"How did you meet him?" he asked with sharp suspicion.

Karen arched her eyebrows at his persistence but again answered honestly. "He was looking for a room. Calvin Muthard sent him here."

"But hadn't you closed the bed-and-breakfast by then?" Charles didn't attempt to hide his annoyance; he had never approved of her opening the house to paying guests.

"Yes." A hint of her thinning patience tightened her tone; Charles chose to ignore.

"You let him stay here even though you had closed the house for the season?"

"That's right."

Anger flushing his cheeks, Charles studied her narrowly. When he spoke again, his voice was low and not at all pleasant. "You were lovers, weren't you?"

Karen's patience snapped, and so did she. "That's none of your business."

"Which means you were," Charles snapped back. "Weren't you?"

"Yes, we were." The cool, controlled response came not from Karen but from the man standing in the doorway to the veranda. "So what?" Paul added, sauntering into the room.

The color deepened in Charles's cheeks, indicating his mounting anger. "You're intruding on a private conversation, Vanzant," Charles said nastily.

"Rude of me, I know," Paul drawled, crossing the room to stand beside Karen. "But since I'm directly involved, I think I'll continue to intrude."

As irritated as Karen was by Charles's audacity in presuming to question her about her private life, Karen felt a jolt of alarm as his breathing increased and his color became mottled. She took a hesitant step toward him. "Charles, are you feeling all right?"

Charles glared at her. "No, I'm not all right." His chest heaved as he inhaled swiftly. "I'd hoped the weekend would be good for me, but I guess it was too much too soon." A thoughtful, almost crafty expression flickered over his face. His voice dwindled to a sigh. "I'm tired."

Really alarmed, Karen rushed to his side. "Do you have any pain?" Her voice was strained by a concern that was obvious to both men. Karen was too busy taking Charles's pulse to notice the smirk of satisfaction he aimed at Paul

"No—" he sighed heavily "—well, just a twinge."

Karen's throat closed. What in the world would she do if Charles suffered another attack right in her kitchen? In an unconsciously revealing move, she turned to Paul. "Will you drive us to the hospital in Portland?"

"Certainly," Paul replied promptly.

"I don't think it's necessary." Charles's voice overlapped Paul's. "At least not yet," he added when he noticed the mildly skeptical look on Paul's face. "It's gone now. I think I just need some peace and quiet for a few days.''

"Are you positive?" Karen asked anxiously.

"Yes," he insisted weakly. "I just need some rest."

The tightness in Karen's throat eased as she saw the color recede from his cheeks. She exhaled a sigh of relief. "Can I get you something?"

"I could drink a cup of decaffeinated coffee," he said tiredly. "If you don't mind?"

"Of course not!" Karen whirled around to get the coffee, and missed the smug look Charles leveled at Paul.

That morning set the pattern for the two weeks that followed, for Charles literally kept Karen on the run. He seldom complained, but then he didn't have to complain. All Charles had to do to get Karen's undivided attention was grimace faintly and moan softly. Karen rarely found more than a few moments to be alone with Paul, and so she didn't notice his expression growing harder and more stern with each passing day.

To Karen's relief, Charles refrained from mentioning her relationship with Paul. In fact, except for the occasional periods when he displayed discomfort, Charles couldn't have been more charming or easier to get along with. His good mood ended with a burst of childish temper at the beginning of the second week of December.

Before they had left Boston, Dr. Rayburn had made arrangements for Charles to consult with a specialist in Portland. Karen had driven Charles into Portland for his first appointment the second week of November. At that time, the doctor had been satisfied with

Charles's progress and had said he would like to see him in a month. Karen set the fuse to Charles's temper by suggesting Paul drive them into Portland so that Charles could keep his appointment.

"Isn't it enough that I have to bear sharing this house with your lover?" Charles shouted at her. "I will be damned if I'll let you coop me up in a car with him!"

Karen backed down. Paul's expression became grim.

"He's using you," Paul said harshly, capturing Karen alone in the hallway as she was putting on her coat the morning of Charles's appointment.

Karen shrugged helplessly. "I know. But he's not well, and I—" Her voice failed when she saw the anger that flashed in Paul's eyes.

"Isn't he?" Paul's eyes glittered behind his narrowed lids. "I'm beginning to have strong doubts about the seriousness of Charles's condition."

Since Karen had doubts of her own, she could hardly argue. Her shoulders rose, then dropped tiredly. "Perhaps the specialist will allow Charles to go back to work and resume more normal activities."

Paul arched one eyebrow. "Will you be present during the examination?"

"Well, no, but—"

Paul cut her off abruptly. "That's what I thought. Which means you'll have no way of knowing what the doctor says to him, will you?" Karen conceded his point by shaking her head slowly. Paul's expression gentled. "Karen, I think it would be to your advantage to have your own consultation with the specialist. For all you know, the doctor may have told him he could return to Boston after the last visit.''

Though Karen didn't want to accept the possibility that Charles was deliberately extending his recuperative period, she knew that he was capable of doing so should it suit his purposes. She simply couldn't comprehend what his purpose could be in this instance. She frowned at Paul. ''But Charles has always said that this is the dullest place on the East Coast. What reason could he have for wanting to remain here?''

''You haven't figured that out yet?'' Paul's lips slanted wryly. ''Charles wants to stay because he wants you.''

Karen blinked in amazement. ''Oh, Paul, that's ridiculous! Charles and I have been divorced for over five years. Why would he suddenly decide he wants me?''

Paul ran a cool but very flattering glance over her gently curved body. ''I can think of many reasons,'' he said dryly, ''because I share them.''

''But he had me and let me go!'' Karen protested.

''Did he really let you go?'' Paul countered. ''Or did you walk away from him?''

''I didn't walk, I ran!'' Karen exclaimed.

''Did he try to stop you or talk you into staying with him?''

Karen lifted her head. ''I didn't give him the opportunity.''

''Precisely.''

Karen still couldn't accept the idea. ''But it's been over five years, Paul,'' she said doggedly.

''Five years of self-indulgence,'' he retorted. ''Five years of who knows how many different women. Five years of instability. And now a heart attack has made him face his own mortality.'' Paul paused, then shot another question at her. ''Has he ever mentioned a current, er . . . relationship?''

Karen sighed as acceptance finally shuddered through her. ''Yes. While he was in the hospital, Charles told me he had recently ended a relationship.'' She moistened her lips, then went on in a whisper, ''He admitted to me that none of the relationships he'd engaged in had been as satisfying for him as our marriage had been.''

''There you go.''

Karen stared at Paul for long seconds. Then she nodded once, sharply. ''I'll talk to the doctor.''

Chapter Twelve

As it turned out, Karen didn't need to consult with the specialist. Charles himself made the meeting unnecessary with the first words out of his mouth on leaving the doctor's office.

"Good news," he said jauntily, clasping her arm to draw her with him toward the door. "The doctor said that if I continue to improve at the same rate I can go back to work after the holidays."

Since she had decided to consult with the specialist, Karen was tugging against the hold he had on her arm, resisting his efforts to get her out of the office. His announcement took all resistance out of her, and she allowed him to lead her from the building to the car.

"Well, isn't that good news?" Charles asked impatiently when she didn't respond immediately.

"Yes, very good news." Karen carefully pried his hand from her arm. "I'm glad he's satisfied with the progress you're making.

"I thought you would be."

Suspicion rose in Karen's mind at his smug tone and expression. It appeared more than a little odd to her that immediately after Paul's suggestion to her about having a talk with the doctor, Charles had suddenly been given good news. Had Charles overheard the discussion between her and Paul earlier? she wondered, frowning as she unlocked the car. He had supposedly been in his room, getting ready to leave for the drive into Portland, but ... Karen slanted a glance at Charles as she slid behind the wheel. Could he have been standing in the upstairs hall, eavesdropping? Though Karen didn't like to believe that Charles would listen in on a private conversation, she knew Charles was capable of listening at keyholes if he thought it to his own advantage.

"Is something wrong?"

Karen blinked. "What?"

"You've been scowling at the steering wheel for several minutes," Charles said. "Is something wrong with it?"

"Oh! No." Smiling faintly, Karen thrust the key into the ignition and started the car. "I was, ah, thinking." And getting nowhere with my thoughts, she added silently. Backing out of the parking space, Karen decided that speculation was pointless regarding her suspicions both about whether Charles had indulged in a little eavesdropping and whether the specialist had in fact given Charles his good news during his previous visit in November.

As she drove out of the lot and into the stream of traffic, Karen mentally shrugged. What Charles was up to, for whatever reason, didn't really matter. In less than a month he'd be returning to Boston. She'd be free, with the time and the opportunity to explore the possibility of a lasting relationship with Paul.

Paul. Karen silently repeated his name, thrilling to the image of him that filled her mind, and nearly missed a streetlight that was turning red. Waiting for the light to change, Karen got lost in a dream of a tall, aristocratic-looking banker. Charles's voice shattered her pleasant musings.

"I want to celebrate. Let's have dinner in the most expensive restaurant in town."

Karen frowned and eased her foot from the brake as the light turned green. She didn't want to have dinner in any restaurant in town, expensive or otherwise. She wanted to go home to Paul. Searching for an excuse to reject his suggestion, she scanned the sky.

"I think I'd just as soon go straight home, Charles," she said reasonably. "I really don't like the look of that sky."

"Oh, come on, Karen. Your boyfriend will be all right on his own for one day." Charles snickered and added, "And I use the term *boy* loosely."

Karen's fingers tightened around the steering wheel. "That's not very funny, Charles." Her voice was as tight as her grip.

"You're damned right it's not funny!" Charles twisted in the seat to glare at her. "The man's almost as old as my father, old enough to be your father. I never realized that you had a father fixation, Karen.'' He paused for breath. Karen opened her mouth to protest, but he didn't let her get a word out. ''Is that why you left me? Was I too young, too modern for you?''

His attack was unwarranted, unfair and grossly incorrect. Karen was suddenly angrier than she'd ever been in her life, so angry she couldn't speak for a moment. Twisting the wheel, she drove onto the access ramp to Interstate 95. She was going too fast, and the car swayed.

''For crying out loud!'' Charles exclaimed. ''Are you trying to land us in a heap by the side of the road?''

Karen eased her foot from the accelerator, then carefully merged with the stream of traffic. She didn't trust herself to speak until the car was moving along smoothly at a legal fifty-five miles per hour.

''Any more remarks like that and I'll happily dump you by the side of the road.'' Karen's voice was harsh; her fingers trembled as they gripped the wheel.

''I could've had another heart attack,'' Charles whined. ''You scared the hell out of me.''

Karen counted to ten, and as she did she counted the number of times Charles had verbally hit her with the heart-attack shtick since she'd brought him to Maine. Memories flashed rapidly across her mind, memories of all the times Charles had frightened her with complaints of shortness of breath, twinges of pain and excessive weariness. The last time had been the night before, while she and Paul had laughed together as they cleaned up the kitchen after dinner. Suddenly Karen felt like the world's most gullible fool.

Damn him! she thought, but corrected herself immediately. No, she should be damning herself! For while it was true that Charles had effortlessly manipulated her for weeks with the threat of another impending attack, she had allowed him to manipulate her, just as she'd allowed him to manipulate her with sweet talk and promises during the years of their marriage.

Hadn't she learned anything in the years since their divorce? Karen asked herself with sharp impatience. She had believed herself mature, adult, independent, but... Karen's lips tightened with self-disdain. Due to her own immature, self-imposed mental state of guilt and remorse because of her relationship with Paul, she had been the perfect patsy for Charles. And as Charles had always been an opportunist by nature, he had immediately identified and capitalized on her weakness. In truth, Karen knew she had earned every second of worry and torment Charles had given her.

"Aren't we going to stop for dinner?" Charles's voice sounded much the same as Mark's when he was pouting and also betrayed the uneasiness he was feeling because of her lengthy silence.

"No, I told you I want to go right home." Karen's tone was vaguely disinterested. She was much too angry to care if Charles was discontent or disappointed. Her eyes narrowed on the road, and the first fat snowflakes plopped onto the windshield. Karen could have used the snow as an excuse but couldn't be bothered.

Obviously aware that her desire to get home had little to do with the weather, Charles didn't mention it, either. In his frustration he took a verbal stab at her, striking her most vulnerable spot.

"He's a grandfather," he sniped nastily.

"So what?" Karen said, unconsciously echoing Paul's bland tone of a few weeks earlier.

"He's too old for you."

Karen shrugged, and that was when Charles struck.

"I'd bet Rand immediately figured it out that you and Grandpa were getting it on." He sneered. "And I'd also bet that by now Rand has painted a pretty lurid picture for Mark." Patently satisfied with the shocked gasp he'd wrenched from her, Charles smiled smugly and settled into his seat.

"Shut up!" Karen's demand lacked strength, for as appalled as she was by his crudity, she was more appalled by the content in his deliberate choice of words.

"Why?" Charles shot back, digging at her vulnerability. "Don't tell me you didn't realize that Rand had to get wise to what was going on? The kid's not stupid, you know." His lips twisted. "Paul betrays himself and you every time he gives you one of those hot, hungry looks." He raked her body with a jealous, thwarted glare. "And you're no better when you look at him. It's obvious to anyone with eyes to see that you and he are lovers. And it's pretty disgusting."

Karen knew that Charles was pulling strings, playing his game of manipulation, and yet she felt sick at the image that rose in her mind. The image was of

Rand, his expression cold with disgust…disgust with her.

No, oh, please, no! The cry of despair rang in her mind. She was in love with Paul, so deeply and irrevocably in love with him that she no longer felt ashamed of the physical relationship they'd shared. In fact, she longed to repeat it. She felt empty and incomplete without Paul beside her at night, making her a part of him by becoming a part of her. She believed Charles's assertion that her feelings were revealed when she looked at Paul; Karen had seen those feelings reflected back to her in Paul's expression. But had Rand noticed, misinterpreted and been disgusted by the proof of what she and Paul were feeling for one another? Karen shuddered at the thought.

"Not a pleasant consideration, is it?"

Oddly, it was the complacent purr of Charles's tone that reactivated Karen's common sense. Another image filled her mind, the image of Rand as he'd looked the day he'd left to go back to school. Rand had hugged Karen and thrust his hand out for Paul's handshake. Rand's expression had revealed love for her and respect for Paul. The memory was clear and revealed Charles's willingness to use any means, even his own son, to attain his desires.

Suddenly sheer fury swept through Karen, dispersing weeks of accumulated doubts and uncertainty. And, just as suddenly, she knew what she had to do. She'd had enough of Charles Mitchell and his machinations.

Her decision made, Karen turned off the interstate at the next exit, circled around and drove onto it again, heading back to Portland.

Alert, his eyes gleaming with victory, Charles favored her with his most dazzling smile. "I knew if you thought about the situation you'd see things my way." His voice was as smooth as glass, his tone all gracious condescension. "I'll have a talk with Rand sometime during the Christmas holidays and explain the circumstances to him."

"Circumstances?" Karen asked, deliberately nudging him into talking himself into a sealed box. "What circumstances?"

"Why concerning you and Vanzant, of course." Charles flicked his hand as if to dismiss the older man. "I'll explain to Rand that this kind of thing is natural for a woman your age, one who has been on her own for too long. Rand's old enough to understand how a lonely woman could be seduced by an older, experienced man." His smile nearly earned him a smack in the face. "But enough of that. I'll take care of that problem at Christmas. Right now, I want to know what restaurant you have in mind for dinner."

Karen was hard-pressed not to laugh out loud. The man's conceit was outweighed only by his gift for self-deception. A woman her age, indeed! She didn't even waste time looking at him.

"I haven't any restaurant in mind, Charles," she said blandly. "I'm driving you to the airport." Though several inches separated them, Karen could actually feel him stiffen.

"Airport?" he repeated starkly. "What for?"

"Why the obvious, Charles." Karen flashed a brilliant smile in his direction. "I'm going to toss you on the first available plane to Boston."

"But the doctor said I was to have two more weeks of recuperation!"

"But he didn't stipulate where, did he?" she countered.

"But my heart!"

"My foot!" Karen spared a glance from the wet, snowy highway to sear him with a disdainful look. Merely returning her gaze to the road was a dismissal. "You have used your health against me for the last time, Charles." Her voice was devoid of compassion. "I'm not responsible for your life or your physical condition—you are." A wry smile curved her lips. "But I'll stop by the doctor's office and ask him if it's safe for you to fly if it will calm your fears."

"I'm not afraid!" Charles said heatedly, sounding exactly like his thirteen-year-old son. "And you don't have to stop by the doctor's office. I wouldn't stay with you now if a dozen specialists advised me not to travel." He hunched down in the bucket seat and thrust his jaw out belligerently. "I can't imagine why I ever considered starting over again with you," he muttered.

"I can't, either," Karen said in amazement. "Because to tell you the truth, Charles, you didn't stand an ice cube's chance in hell . . . Paul Vanzant or not."

Several hours later, Karen was again driving on Interstate 95, and though the snowfall was growing steadily heavier, her spirits were as light as a spring breeze. Most of those hours had been spent anxiously waiting at the airport, as they had learned on arrival that the Boston flight was fully booked. For a few moments, Charles had reverted to his attitude of superiority, but after one close look at Karen's implacable expression he'd agreed to wait on standby. To her relief, when the Boston flight was called, there were three no-shows, probably due to the weather. When the plane took off, Charles was on it.

Peering at the highway through the curtain of lacy white flakes, Karen smiled and decided she loved the cold, wet stuff. Her fingers were icy and her toes were cold, but Karen didn't mind; she was eagerly looking forward to a warm bed and an even warmer Paul Vanzant. Karen laughed aloud at the prospect.

"Where the hell are they?" Unaware of growling the question aloud, Paul followed it up with a muttered string of curses that would have curled a maiden lady's eyelashes.

Prowling through the house like a wild thing, he strode to the long, narrow windows facing the road. Pulling the drapes aside, Paul frowned at the unbroken ground cover of white obscuring the lines between the driveway and the front lawn.

Speculations and fears, each more chilling than the rising wind, tumbled through his mind, freezing Paul in place. Had Karen had car trouble? Had there been an accident on the slick road? Had she been injured? Had Charles prevailed and talked Karen into spending the night in Portland—with him?

"I'll ruin the son of a—" Paul clamped his lips together. He knew that driving on the thin layer of snow had to be a nightmare. Part of him was hoping she'd decided not to attempt the trip until the storm was over and road crews had cleared the highway. Yet another more possessive part of Paul rebelled at the idea of Karen being snowbound with Charles.

Paul knew, had known after being in the house one day, that Charles was determined to win Karen back again. And Paul was equally determined to prevent Charles from succeeding.

"Karen's mine." This time Paul was fully aware of speaking out loud and of the harsh sound of his voice in the too-quiet room. Why hasn't she called? he asked himself for the dozenth time. His narrowed gaze scanned the white landscape. His patience thinned. "Dammit! If she doesn't call or get home soon, I'm going after her!" The vow was no sooner out of Paul's mouth than the eerie glow of a car's headlights pierced the hazy swirl of white. Paul was across the room and to the door before the car made the turn into the driveway.

"Where the hell have you been?"

Paul's rough voice was like a crooning caress to Karen. Swinging the car door shut, Karen trudged through the snow, unconcerned with the cold wet soaking her shoes. A pang speared through her chest at the sight of Paul moving toward her, his tall frame outlined by the blaze of light from the house. He looked so natural coming from her house, so perfectly right.

"I've been tying up a few loose ends," she replied, a carefree smile curving her lips.

"What?" Paul started to return her smile, but before she could say another word he frowned and glanced around sharply. "Where's Charles?" Draping a sweater-clad arm around her damp shoulders, he turned and hurried her into the welcoming warmth of the house.

Karen didn't answer until the solid thunk of the closing door shut out the keening wail of the wind. "Charles is on a plane headed for Boston."

Paul had placed his hands on her shoulders to help her remove her coat. At her response, his fingers flexed, digging into the material. "On a plane," he repeated with soft incredulity. "But how? Why?"

Slipping out of her coat, Karen whirled to face him. "How? Very simply. I drove him to the airport and waited until the plane took off." Her head lifted with an unconscious regality. "Why? Because I was thoroughly fed up with his manipulative, disruptive influence. In short, I tossed him out."

The garment he was clutching forgotten, Paul stared at her in disbelief for a moment, his lips twitching against a smile. "But was that safe?" he asked somberly, winning the battle with his mouth.

"I hope so." Karen drew in a deep breath as she turned to the hall phone table. "And I intend to find out right now."

Gazing down at the jacket still clasped in his hands, Paul absently hung it in the closet. "You're calling his doctor?" he asked as she punched in the Portland number.

"Yes. I didn't get the opportunity to talk to him earlier...." She broke off, then said, "Oh, yes, this is Karen Mitchell. I'd like to speak to Dr. Jennaue, please. Yes, it is important." While she was waiting, Karen tapped her fingernails on the smooth tabletop and glanced at Paul. "I'll tell you all about it after I've spoken to the doctor."

Paul inclined his head. "All right."

"There's a problem, Ms. Mitchell?" Dr. Jennaue asked with direct briskness.

"I'm not sure, Doctor." Karen's hand tightened reflexively on the telephone receiver. "I, er, put Charles on a plane for Boston a while ago, and I wanted your professional opinion on whether that was a safe thing to do," she said quickly, then immediately held her breath.

"Safe? Why shouldn't it be safe? I told Mr. Mitchell last month that he could resume normal activities—within reason, of course. Surely he told you?" Impatience could be heard in the doctor's tone.

Karen's eyes narrowed on hearing confirmation of her suspicions. Charles had been lying to her for weeks—forever! Gathering her thoughts, she answered, "Ah, yes, but I wasn't positive if flying came under the heading of reasonable activities. Thank you, Doctor, and I'm sorry I bothered you."

"No bother at all," the doctor said, then contradicted himself by hanging up without the courtesy of a farewell.

As her finger depressed the disconnect button, Karen gazed at Paul. "Charles was lying. The doctor told him to resume normal activities during his visit last month." As she relayed the information to Paul, she punched in another number, long-distance this time.

"You're calling the school?" Paul correctly guessed.

"Yes."

It required a few moments, but finally Rand's anxious voice traveled across miles of telephone wire.

"Mom, is something wrong?"

"No!" Karen said at once. "No, Rand," she went on in a calm voice. "I just thought you should know that, with the doctor's permission, I took your father to the airport to catch the late-afternoon plane to Boston."

There was dead silence for several seconds. During those agonizing moments, Karen fought against the urge to launch into defensive speech, explaining to her son that she couldn't tolerate his father's presence a minute longer. The inner battle was hard-fought, but she won.

"You kicked him out, didn't you?" Rand demanded.

Karen thought about evasion and immediately rejected the thought; that was Charles's method, not hers. "Yes, Rand, I kicked him out." She held her breath and waited for condemnation.

"About time, too." Rand's voice didn't crack at all; his tone had the depth of growing maturity. "I was wonderin' how long it would take before you got fed up with his bellyachin'."

Tears rushed to Karen's eyes, and she blinked against the sting. A long, muscular arm circled her waist, and a warm male body pressed reassuringly against hers, giving her the strength to whisper her son's name. "Oh, Rand."

"I—I love Dad, Mom, but that doesn't mean I can't see him for what he is, you know."

"I know." Karen made no attempt to stem the flow of tears running down her face. Obviously misreading the situation, Paul tightened his arm protectively and pressed the strength of his body closer to hers. Literally surrounded by understanding and protection, Karen suddenly laughed. "I'm so proud of you, Rand. You're going to be a fantastic man."

"Yeah, I know." Like most young people uncomfortable with praise, Rand reverted to wisecracks. "Ain't you the lucky one?"

"Yes, darling, I really am," Karen responded softly, seriously. Rand was quiet for a moment, and she heard him swallow. When he spoke again, his voice was husky.

"Is Mr. Vanzant still there?"

Karen's feeling of well-being wavered, and she stiffened. Again she considered and rejected evasion. "Yes, he is."

"Good deal," Rand said briskly. "I worry about you being all alone up there... and, ah... I like Mr. Vanzant, Mom. I kinda think he's good for you. Will you tell him I said hello?"

Karen didn't attempt to conceal the relief she felt at receiving her son's words of approval. "Yes, of course I will," she choked out. "I'd better let you get back to whatever you were doing. I'll see you in two weeks."

"Yeah, Christmas! I can't wait." Rand laughed. Then he said softly, "And Mom? Don't worry about Mark. I'll explain everything to him."

Wondering if the day would ever come when her son ceased to amaze her, Karen cleared her throat. "Thank you, Rand. I love you very much."

"Yeah, I know." Rand's voice was husky again. "I love you back. Bye, Mom."

Karen's voice trembled as she said goodbye, her hand trembled as she cradled the receiver, and her eyelashes trembled as she blinked against a fresh surge of tears.

"Problems?" Paul murmured, tightening his arm around her waist even more.

Snuggling closer to his warmth, Karen shook her head. "Just the opposite." She sniffled and laughed. "My boy's growing up, Paul. Not only does he understand his father and accept him for what he is, but Rand understands the situation between you and me."

"Indeed?" Paul moved his hips slightly, making her aware of the fullness of his arousal.

"Yes!" Karen gasped, shivering in response. "He— Rand said he's glad you are here with me." Her breathing grew erratic as he slowly moved his hips. "Um, he said he likes you and thinks you're good for me. Oh!" She gasped again as his free hand sought her breast.

"Rand's a bright, savvy kid and I like him, too." Relaxing his arm, Paul turned her, drawing her body into intimate contact with his. "And I like Mark." Lowering his head, he lightly touched his mouth to her slightly parted lips. "And I like you best of all," he whispered, wrenching a moan from her by piercing her mouth with the tip of his tongue.

"Oh, Paul." Despite her wet, cold toes, Karen was suddenly burning up, on fire for him. Curling her arms around his waist, she arched her body into the heat of his. A sound of hunger murmured deep in her throat when he stroked his tongue along her lower lip. "Oh, Paul, I ache for you!" she admitted in a whispery cry, past the point of sensuous game-playing.

"And you can obviously feel how much I need you," he muttered, nipping gently at her lip. "So," he murmured, laughter edging his tone, "what are we doing standing here in the hallway?"

"Good question." Stepping back, Karen smiled and slid her hand into his. "It's been a long, eventful day."

Paul didn't have to be coaxed. Spinning around, he strode to the stairs, tugging her with him. As they mounted the stairs, he slanted a look at her. His dark eyes glittered with promise. "The way I'm feeling now, I think I can guarantee that it will be an even longer, much more eventful night."

Weeks of separation followed by weeks of being together without the opportunity to actually be together had created a voracious mutual hunger approaching starvation. In a replay of their first time together, they left the bedroom door standing wide open in their haste to touch, taste, caress and tear the clothes from one another's body. The bed was a haven eagerly sought.

Paul's mouth was hot and hungry on Karen's as his body joined with hers in a joyous rush. It was wild and wonderful. It was electric and sweet. It was homecoming. Satisfaction was swiftly attained and just as swiftly forgotten in the renewing heat of desire.

Paul's stamina was startling, and Karen found the strength to match his. Paul was dominant, Karen submissive. In turn, Karen became the aggressor, Paul the supplicant. Their reward was exhausted repletion.

While the snowstorm raged outside, whipping the roiling waves into a white-crested fury, rattling windows and blanketing the land in a coat of pristine white, Karen and Paul slept deeply, wrapped in the warmth of one another's arms.

Sprawled luxuriously across Paul's silver-flecked, dark-haired chest, Karen woke to the lulling sound of a calm sea and the whitish light of a snow-covered world. Feeling tired but contented, she snuggled closer to Paul's warmth and rubbed her cheek against the springy curls of his silky chest hair.

"Good morning." Paul's gently expelled breath ruffled the hair on top of her head.

Karen's lips curved into a satisfied smile as she tilted her head to the side to gaze up at him. "Good morning. Did you sleep well?"

"Hmm." Paul's eyes gleamed as he dipped his lightly bristled chin in a nod. "I feel terrific. How about you?"

Karen's smile deepened. "I feel wonderful." She paused for effect. "And utterly exhausted."

Paul's lips curved into a smile of supreme male satisfaction. "I did promise you an eventful night."

"You kept your promise." She was quiet a moment as memory stirred. Then she laughed with delight.

Paul's smile widened. "What's so amusing?"

"I just remembered something Charles said."

A frown banished Paul's smile. "What did he say?" he asked, his arms tightening around her possessively.

Karen's laughter bubbled. "He said you were too old for me."

Instead of joining in her laughter as she'd expected him to, Paul grew somber. Her laughter fading, Karen gazed up at him.

"What is it?" she asked, beginning to frown.

"Charles was right, Karen." Paul sighed. "I am too old for you."

Chapter Thirteen

Paul!" Rearing back, Karen attempted to free herself from his embrace. Her expression and her tone revealed sheer incredulity. "How can you say that after the night we just spent together!"

Refusing to release her completely, Paul eased her from his chest to the mattress beside him. "I can say that because it's true." Leaning over her, he raised a hand to rake long fingers through her hair, tangling them in the disheveled mass. "Look at you," he murmured, searing a dark-eyed gaze the length of her nude body. "Do you know what I see when I look at you?"

Karen's throat was too tight to allow the passage of words. A sinking sensation invaded her stomach. With her mind's eye she could see herself as she imagined Paul saw her. And what she saw was a woman who looked every one of her thirty-seven years. She loved good food, and the results were firmly packed around her hips. She had borne two children, and her body bore the marks. Her breasts, though still firm, no longer retained the high thrust of youth. Her hands revealed her willingness to work and showed none of the soft silkiness of idle pampering.

Never before had Karen been dissatisfied with her appearance. She had never been beautiful. But she had always been attractive, and that had been enough until now. Now Karen longed to be beautiful...for Paul. Beginning to hurt deep inside, Karen shook her head. "No, what do you see when you look at me?"

"I see a woman in the full bloom of life—lovely, vibrant, gloriously alive. And you deserve a man like yourself to build a future with." Paul's sigh and smile hurt her heart. "Karen, I am well into middle age. I haven't all that much future to offer."

With his hand buried in her hair, it was difficult for Karen to move without causing a sharp tug of pain in her scalp. But she did, ignoring the tears in her eyes as she struggled to sit up. "Paul, that's ridiculous!" she cried indignantly. "You literally wore me out last night!" she admitted, blushing.

"Thank you for that." Paul's voice was husky with emotion. Raising his hand, he traced her features with his fingertips as if imprinting the feel of her on his skin. "But there was a reason for my prowess last night. After weeks of missing you, then being near you but denied the right to touch you, I was starving for you."

"No, no," Karen protested, shaking her head vigorously. "That might explain last night, but what about that first time? You were every bit as . . . as aggressive the first time we made love.''

Jolting up, Paul grasped her by the shoulders. ''Of course I was aggressive!'' he said in a gritty voice. ''I had not been with a woman in over six years!'' The instant the words were out of his mouth, Paul bit down hard on his lip as if he wished he could bite back the confession. ''Oh, damn!'' he groaned, wincing at the sight of her baffled expression. His fingers flexed convulsively in the soft flesh of her shoulders. ''Karen, listen to me. Until the day I met you, I honestly believed that I was impotent.''

Impotent! Karen blinked. Paul? Karen laughed; she couldn't help it. He had to be kidding! But he wasn't, and she knew it. Her laughter held a note of hysteria. ''I'm sorry,'' she gasped, fighting against the natural succession of tears after the laughter. ''But, Paul, I can't believe . . .'' Karen's voice faded.

Paul sighed and loosened his grip on her shoulders. ''Believe it, Karen. I was celibate for over six years, not by choice but because I felt no stirrings of desire for any woman—until I met you.'' Leaning toward her, he kissed her with a reverence that brought tears to her eyes. ''And I've been thanking God for our meeting, and for you, ever since.''

Sitting naked on the bed, tears trickling down her face, Karen felt weak with compassion for him and grateful for being the woman who had been there at his reawakening. Sniffing, she brushed impatiently at her wet cheeks. ''I'd like you to know that, although it was by choice, I had been celibate for over five years before I met you.''

His fingers tightened again on her tender skin, making a lie of his protest. "You shouldn't have been! You're too young to deny yourself the pleasure of love." His lips twisted into a wry smile. "And that's what I've been trying to tell you. I am past the age of giving you the pleasure you deserve."

Suddenly impatient with him, Karen shook off his hands. "You are not old!" She shouted the denial, yet at that moment, with his somber expression revealing every scoring line of experience, Paul did indeed look his age.

"But, my love," he murmured in an aching tone, "I am too old for you. Do you realize that I have a son older than you are?"

Her eyes widening with disbelief, Karen skimmed her gaze down his body, admiring the trim, well-toned look of him. Impossible, she decided. Even though he had told her he'd never see fifty again, Paul simply could not be old enough to have fathered a child who was now forty or near enough to it to make little difference. "Paul, really..." she began, only to break off at the sound of his introspective murmur.

"I was seventeen."

"What?"

Paul shuddered and glanced away from her. "Nothing." With startling suddenness, he sprang from the bed. "I'm hungry."

Karen's eyes narrowed. "Paul, you simply can't let it go at that! What happened when you were seventeen?"

Paul had started for the bathroom; he didn't stop. His only response was an impatient shrug that rippled over his muscular shoulders and down his attractively tapered back.

"Paul!" Karen's tone was laced with the same note of command she occasionally had to use on her children. And she derived the same result; Paul stopped in his tracks.

"Over breakfast, Karen. Okay?"

Karen resigned herself to the delay with a sighed "Yes, Paul."

The bowed windows in the dining alcove framed a Christmas-card scene of sparkling white snow blanketing the landscape and mantling bushes and tree branches. After her delighted cry on her first sight of it, Karen didn't notice. She was too busy studying Paul.

Pondering his intriguing murmur, she barely touched the food he'd helped her prepare. Sipping her coffee, Karen bided her time until he'd finished chewing the last bite of his breakfast. She pounced the instant he placed his napkin on the table.

"You were seventeen?" she prompted softly.

Paul's smile contained genuine, if wry, amusement. "I should have added tenaciousness to your list of attributes."

Karen stared at him stoically.

"Right." Paul nodded sharply. "I was seventeen when my son Peter was born." He smiled as her eyes grew wide with surprise. "He was legitimate. His mother and I were man and wife."

Karen glared at him. "I assumed you were! But you were so young. How in the world—" Karen stopped speaking simply because the question was stupid—she knew how!

"Karen, are you sure you want to hear the story of my life?" Paul grimaced. "I assure you it is very dull fare."

Karen indicated the snowy world beyond the windows. "I'm not going anywhere. And I don't believe you could be dull if you worked at it."

"I fell in love with Carolyn the first time I saw her, the day her family moved into the house on the small estate next to ours." Though Paul began his recitation in a droning voice, his tone gradually changed, becoming soft and pensive. "I was hiding behind the line of yews that separated the properties, curious about the new neighbors." His lips curved in a tender smile of remembrance. "I was six years old. Carolyn was five. She had long, shining hair and she was the most beautiful creature my young eyes had ever seen. I immediately fell into a state of adoration and stayed there."

Karen experienced a stab of emotion too similar to jealousy to be examined. Carefully controlling her expression, she merely arched her eyebrows questioningly.

Paul laughed. "Incredible, isn't it?" Since he didn't expect a response, he didn't wait for one. "I loved her. No—" He shook his head. "I worshiped the air she breathed." Paul shut his eyes, and his expression sent a shaft of pain into Karen's heart. "She was slender and delicate and unpredictable and so stunningly beautiful."

A mirror image of herself flashed into Karen's mind, and she had to bite her lip to keep from crying out for him to stop. She didn't want to hear anymore; she wanted to run away and hide. But even as she berated herself for having insisted he tell her his story, she urged him to continue. "Go on."

Paul complied like an automaton. "Carolyn discovered me peering at her from behind the yews, and from that day on we were practically inseparable. We were best friends until the year I was sixteen and she was fifteen." He smiled sadly. "Then we became lovers."

"Oh, Paul." Karen's voice was soft with understanding and compassion.

Paul didn't seem to hear. "We were so very young and so very dumb." He shrugged. "We knew nothing about birth control, of course, and, unprotected, Carolyn conceived almost immediately." His smile held the wisdom gained during the forty-year interval. "I'm sure you can imagine how the news was received by our parents."

"Oh, yes," Karen murmured, thinking of Rand.

"Her mother went directly into a decline, her father threatened to, er, dismember me." Paul winced at the mere idea. "My mother cried off and on for a week, my father retired to his study, refusing to look at me. But in the end, Carolyn and I were married—with their blessing. I was in my senior year of high school when Peter was born six months later." A soft glow entered Paul's eyes at the mention of his son's name. "As had happened with his mother, I adored my son from the instant the nurse unwrapped his blanket to present him to me minutes after he made his appearance in the world." He chuckled. "I still adore him, and that devil knows it."

Karen had to swallow before she could articulate. "And your daughter?"

"Ahhh, Nicole," Paul responded in a loving murmur. Then he gave a short, helpless laugh. "As luck would have it, Carolyn didn't conceive again until after Peter's ninth birthday. I had thought it would be nice to have a daughter, but I couldn't imagine..." Paul's voice faded on a note of wonder, then came back with a note of awe. "Though I wouldn't have believed it possible, my daughter was exquisite from birth, even more beautiful than her mother." He exhaled a heartfelt sigh. "Nicole was in a car accident several years ago and was left with a scar on her right cheek, but she's still exquisitely beautiful." He smiled into Karen's eyes. "Her husband, J.B., would die for her without a second thought, he loves her that much."

"As you loved her mother?" Karen's voice revealed a longing ache. She breathed a sigh of relief when he appeared not to have noticed.

"Yes, until—" Paul broke off abruptly to change the subject. "Is there any coffee left?"

Alert to his evasive ploy yet cautioning herself to be patient, Karen slid her chair away from the table. "There's a fresh pot. I'll get it." Grasping the carafe, she stood up, frowning when he pushed his chair back.

"We may as well clear the table," he said in answer to her silent, frowning query.

"You were saying you loved Carolyn until..."
Karen prompted some ten minutes later when they
were again seated at the neatly cleared table.

Avoiding her direct gaze, Paul sipped his steaming
coffee, then shifted to glance at the carpet. A sensuous smile curved his lips. "This dining area holds
some very pleasant memories for me," he murmured.

Karen had a fleeting vision of herself, naked and
eager, wantonly stretched out on the spot where his
dark-eyed gaze rested, and choked on a swallow of
coffee. "Yes, well, ah—" She cleared her throat. "Are
you digressing?"

"No, I'm stalling," Paul admitted wryly.

With the sudden realization that she really had no
right to probe into his past, Karen reached across the
table to clasp his hand. "Paul, I'm sorry. We'll discuss something else. The snow, the coming holidays,
the—"

"Karen, shut up." Paul's voice was low, rich with
his appreciation of her understanding. "I loved Carolyn until the day I found out that she was unfaithful
to me, had been unfaithful to me for over ten years.
That was over six years ago." His eyes narrowed and
he watched her closely, waiting for her reaction. He
didn't wait very long.

Karen's eyes widened as she absorbed the enormity
of what he'd said. "You mean," she breathed, "that
it was on learning of her infidelity that you became—"

"Yes." Paul spoke quickly, interrupting her before
she could say the hated word.

"Did you consult a doctor?"

Paul's spine grew rigid, and he lifted his head. "No."

Karen was appalled at his unequivocal reply. "But Paul—" she began in protest, but again he cut her off.

"I didn't need a doctor, Karen," he said harshly. "Very likely because, for a long time, the last thing I wanted was intimate contact with a woman—any woman."

Karen didn't respond; she couldn't. She had to concentrate on merely breathing. She hurt all over, for herself but more intensely for Paul. What she would finally have said in the event she found both breath and voice Karen was never to know, for at that moment, in an eerie repeat of another time they'd been alone in the alcove, the phone rang.

"I'll get it!" Grateful for the diversion, Karen scrambled to her feet and fled to the kitchen wall phone. Without ever having heard the voice before, Karen knew at once that it belonged to Paul's son, Peter.

"Ms. Mitchell?" His voice was deep and dark and incredibly sexy. "This is Peter Vanzant. May I speak to my father, please?"

"Yes, of course," Karen said, picturing him in her mind as a younger version of Paul. She decided she liked him, sight unseen. "Just a moment, please." She turned to find Paul watching her, his expression tense, revealing. Karen knew his fear was that the call concerned Charles. Her smile reassuring, she held out the receiver. "For you," she murmured. "It's your son."

Karen started to move away after handing Paul the phone, but he slid an arm around her waist and drew her tightly against him. As he held the receiver loosely, she couldn't help but overhear the conversation.

"Yes, Peter?"

"Dad, J.B. called a few moments ago. Nicole's in labor."

Paul's only reaction was the compulsive tightening of the arm encircling Karen's waist and the terseness of his tone. "Is there a problem?"

"No. It's early, but only by two weeks. J.B. just wanted to let us know."

"All right, Peter. Thanks for calling."

"You flying to Fort Worth, Dad?"

The inflection in Peter's voice reached Karen with revealing clarity; Peter knew his father very well. Paul's smile was wry. "Yes, Peter, I'll be flying to Fort Worth."

"That's what I thought. Give Nicole and J.B. our love and tell them Patricia and I will be bringing little Paul out to meet his cousin the day after Christmas. And, Dad, call us the minute the baby arrives."

"Of course, Peter."

There was more. Paul asked after Peter's wife and son, but Karen was tuned out, her mind numbed by the realization that Paul was leaving. And although she understood his desire to be with his youngest child at the birth of her first baby, Karen felt frozen by the possibility that once he left Paul might not return.

Her fear grew during the next few hours as Paul swiftly and efficiently booked airline reservations for his flight to Fort Worth and prepared to leave. His remote withdrawal reinforced the possibility, changing it to a probability.

In her determination not to emulate Charles by attempting to force the issue or be manipulative, Karen promised herself she would not pressure Paul by asking if he was planning to come back to her. And she maintained her resolve until he was ready to walk out the door; then she broke her promise to herself with a gush of blurted words.

"Will you be coming back?"

"I don't think that would be wise, Karen." Though Paul's eyes were tender, his tone was adamant. As she stared at him, a thousand arguments rushed through Karen's mind. One word found its way to her lips.

"Why?"

Paul's chest moved as he exhaled deeply. "It wouldn't be fair to you." He held up a hand to silence her when she would have protested. "I have a memory, an image of you in my mind that torments me. The memory is of the first day we met, when you sat across the table from me while in the kitchen. You said, 'I love babies' when I told you I have one grandchild and another on the way. The image in my mind is of the expression of longing on your face." As he had earlier that morning, Paul reached out to trace her features with his fingertips. "I'm past the age of starting another family, Karen, even if I were certain I could, which I'm not."

"Oh, Paul, I don't—" Karen began.

"I am fifty-six years old, Karen!" Paul said harshly. "And, as I told you before, that doesn't leave much of a future to offer you."

"Dammit, Paul!" Karen exploded, forgetting her determination not to apply pressure in her fear of losing him. "When you arrived here the day after Thanksgiving, you told me you thought you were falling in love with me," she said, grasping his hand to hold it to her cheek. "Well, I don't think I'm falling in love with you—I know I'm in love with you." She paused for breath, taking courage from the light of emotion her confession of love ignited in his eyes, but hurried on before he could respond. "And as to the future, no one ever knows how much or how little we have of that. When I married Charles, the future seemed as never-ending as youth. Well, I'm now past the age of believing in forever spring, and though I know I can be content without ever having another baby, I'm not as certain I can ever again be content without having you." Falling silent, Karen clutched his hand and waited breathlessly for his reaction.

Paul closed his eyes as if he were in pain. When he opened them again, they were suspiciously bright. Moving her hand, he slid his palm to the back of her head; then, tangling his fingers in her hair, he drew her mouth to his. His kiss was hard and hungry and desperate. Karen barely had time to respond before he released her abruptly and turned to pull the door open.

"I must go now or I'll miss my plane." His voice was husky with emotion. He stepped outside, then turned to look at her, absorb her, with intense dark eyes. "I'm still not sure, but I'll think about everything you said." Paul hesitated, took another step into the glistening snow, then turned to stare at her once more. "But there is one thing that I'm now absolutely sure of," he said softly. "I do love you, Karen— deeply, maturely, in a way I never loved Carolyn."

Leaving her that one precious gift, Paul turned and strode to his car.

Why doesn't he call me? Please, God, make him call me. Karen was getting used to the litany. It had run through her mind continuously for three excruciatingly long days, ever since Paul's departure four days before.

Throughout those four days, Karen had made a production out of busy work. She had laundered literally everything in the house that would fit into the clothes washer. Every room in the large house was spotless and gleaming with a fresh coat of polish. She had even tackled the detested job of cleaning the kitchen cabinets. She had been anxious to do anything and everything to keep her mind as well as her hands occupied. But after four days of industrious labor, though her house was in order, Karen's mind was in a muddle of uncertainty and fear.

And in a strange way, even in her fear of losing Paul, Karen understood and sympathized with the position he had taken. Karen also knew that there was more, much more involved in his decision than the span of years separating them.

Though proud, Karen knew Paul was a man of deep loyalties. Because he had loved, he had persevered with his marriage even after learning of his wife's infidelity. Because he was proud, Paul had borne the fear of impotence in stoic, if misguided, silence. Because he was loyal, he had endured alone while keeping his family together.

Karen acknowledged sadly that she loved Paul because of all his fine qualities, even though they might prove the reason she would lose him. The paradox was nearly unbearable.

Unabashed tears glistening in his dark eyes, Paul stood at the nursery window, staring in awe at the tiny form of his new granddaughter. Like her mother before her, the infant was exquisite in her perfection. But the cost of her entrance into the world had been high— almost too high, for while fighting to give life to her daughter, Nicole had come perilously close to losing her own.

As to the future, no one knows how much or how little we have of that.

Paul heard Karen's voice as clearly as if she stood beside him in the hospital corridor. *I love you.* Paul wasn't sure if his silent message was meant for the tiny bundle in the small nursery basket or the woman who commanded his every thought and emotion. But then, it really didn't matter. The message applied to both.

By late afternoon of the fourth day, for want of something to do, Karen was reduced to checking her food staples and writing a grocery list. She was bent over a piece of paper on the kitchen counter, about to add baking powder to the list, when she heard the unmistakable sound of a car pulling into the driveway. For an instant, she froze. Then the pencil went sailing into the air as Karen spun to make a mad dash to the door. Hoping, yet afraid to hope, she swung the door open.

"Paul." Every hope, every dream, every aching ounce of love Karen felt for him was wrapped within the whisper of his name.

Looking far less urbane, sophisticated and intimidating but infinitely more relaxed, freer and younger than Karen had ever seen him, Paul smiled, strode into the house and swept her into his arms. His kiss was deep and hungry and spoke eloquently of his need of her. Karen reveled in being crushed beneath his demanding mouth and moaned a soft protest when he raised his head and stepped back. As he moved, he caught her hand with his, as if not wanting to lose contact entirely. Gazing at him, Karen felt her heart flutter at the emotion burning in his dark eyes. Her pulses leaped with his first words to her.

"I want to try to make a baby with you." Paul's voice was low but firm with certainty.

"Is this a proposal of marriage?" Karen asked in a dry, crackling whisper.

Paul's smile held the promise of heaven and the glitter of devilry. "I guess it must be, because I feel positive that Rand would never forgive me if I suggested anything less than marriage."

Wanting to cry, wanting to laugh, and in the end doing both, Karen managed to ask, "And Rand's opinion is important to you?"

Paul replied at once. "Of course, as is the opinion of Mark and Peter and Patricia and Nicole and J.B., and little Paul and my darling new granddaughter." His smile and tone deepened. "Their opinions are very important—for the future."

* * *

"Catch it, Paul!" Mark called excitedly, jumping up and down in the sand near the water's edge.

"You'll never make it!" Rand whooped, proud of the toss he'd made.

The bright orange Frisbee arced high against a brilliant blue spring sky before diving to earth inches from the blanket Karen was sitting on. Scrambling to her feet, she swooped down and plucked it from the sand an instant before Paul came to a panting halt in front of her.

"They're trying to kill me," he gasped, indicating her laughing sons with a backward toss of his head. "Me, the father of their unborn brother or sister!" His teasing eyes lowered to the barely discernible bulge in Karen's jeans.

Controlling her own bubbling laughter, Karen managed a concerned "tsk-tsk" and a frown. "Correct me if I'm wrong, Mr. Vanzant," she said, biting her lip, "but weren't you the one who suggested the game in the first place?"

Paul flicked his hand dismissively. "That's beside the point, Mrs. Vanzant. I hardly expected—"

"Hey, when do we eat?" Rand shouted, drowning out his stepfather's complaint.

"Soon," Karen called, releasing her pent-up laughter. The happy sound wafted along on the warm, balmy air, drawing an exchange of contented grins from Rand and Mark.

Paul groaned, very loudly. "I suppose you now expect me to grill the hot dogs and hamburgers for dinner?" He arched one dark brow at her arrogantly.

Karen tapped the Frisbee against her thigh as she contemplated his question. Then she smiled nicely and fluttered her eyelashes. "Surely you don't expect me, in my delicate condition, to stand over a hot, smoky charcoal grill?" she asked sweetly.

Paul made a very unsophisticated face at her. "If the delicate lady will remember, I did offer to take the family out for dinner," he reminded her smoothly.

"Go out to eat on Memorial Day?" Karen widened her eyes in feigned shock. "Why—why, that's positively un-American!"

"Yeah, right." Paul said, imitating Rand's tone perfectly.

Karen's joyous laughter rang out again. "God, I love you, Paul!" she gasped.

Catching her by the waist, Paul swung her into the air, then pulled her into his arms when he set her down again. "You know what? I love you, too."

"Are you two gonna spend the whole holiday making mush or are we gonna eat sometime soon?" Rand groused as he stomped through the sand toward them.

"Yeah, anyway, I'm hungry," Mark seconded, trailing his idol.

"Yeah, anyway," Paul mimicked, bending to drop a swift kiss on Karen's mouth. "Okay, you win. I'll cook." He stole another kiss before glancing at the boys. "But you kids can haul the food and assorted necessities out to the grill. Hop to it!"

With cries of "Yes, sir" and "You got it," the boys sprinted toward the house.

Returning his undivided attention to Karen, Paul smiled in satisfaction. A shiver tiptoed down her spine at the gleam that sprang into his eyes.

"Paul," she laughed, "are you thinking what I think you're thinking?"

"What else?" He laughed with her. "And if we were alone..." His voice trailed off suggestively.

"But we're not," she reminded him, surging up to give him a quick kiss.

Paul's hand snaked up to grasp her hair, holding her still for a soul-stirring kiss. "I can wait," he murmured against her lips, laughing softly as she shivered in response. He kissed her again, deeply this time. When he lifted his head, his expression was somber, almost reverent. "As long as I know you're here, mine, only mine, I can wait." Working his free hand between them, he placed his palm on her gently rounded belly. "We have our entire future before us. Anticipation will sweeten our private moments together."

* * * * *

The passionate saga that brought you SARAH and
ELIZABETH continues in the compelling,
unforgettable story of

Catherine

MAURA SEGER

An independent and ambitious woman earns the disapproval of Boston society when she discovers passion and
love with Irishman Evan O'Connel.

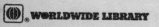

Silhouette Romance™

Legendary Lovers Trilogy

BY DEBBIE MACOMBER....

ONCE UPON A TIME, in a land not so far away, there lived a girl, Debbie Macomber, who grew up dreaming of castles, white knights and princes on fiery steeds. Her family was an ordinary one with a mother and father and one wicked brother, who sold copies of her diary to all the boys in her junior high class.

One day, when Debbie was only nineteen, a handsome electrician drove by in a shiny black convertible. Now Debbie knew a prince when she saw one, and before long they lived in a two-bedroom cottage surrounded by a white picket fence.

As often happens when a damsel fair meets her prince charming, children followed, and soon the two-bedroom cottage became a four-bedroom castle. The kingdom flourished and prospered, and between soccer games and car pools, ballet classes and clarinet lessons, Debbie thought about love and enchantment and the magic of romance.

One day Debbie said, "What this country needs is a good fairy tale." She remembered how well her diary had sold and she dreamed again of castles, white knights and princes on fiery steeds. And so the stories of Cinderella, Beauty and the Beast, and Snow White were reborn....

Look for Debbie Macomber's *Legendary Lovers* trilogy from Silhouette Romance: *Cindy and the Prince* (January, 1988); *Some Kind of Wonderful* (March, 1988); *Almost Paradise* (May, 1988). Don't miss them!

SRT-1

AUTHOR OF *FAMILY FORTUNES*

ELAINE BISSELL

She lived without fear and favor...
and belonged to no one but herself

A gripping saga about a brilliant, strong-willed woman who, determined to build a successful media empire, is sustained by power and ambition until she meets a man who offers the missing element in her life—romance and happiness.

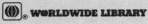

Silhouette Special Edition

COMING NEXT MONTH

#445 THROUGH ALL ETERNITY—Sondra Stanford
Upon colliding with luscious Lila Addison, big Jeffrey Chappel found the former model kind to strangers but cautious about commitment. He vowed to win her precious trust, but could he truly offer her his own heart?

#446 NEVER LET GO—Sherryl Woods
Though Dr. Justin Whitmore acted hard as nails, hospital psychologist Mallory Blake had glimpsed his softer side. As professional awe turned to personal ardor, Mallory longed to crack Justin's icy facade—and rush right into his heart.

#447 SILENT PARTNER—Celeste Hamilton
Fiercely independent Melissa Chambers needed bucks, not brainstorms, to launch her new restaurant. But headstrong Hunt Kirkland, her far-from-silent partner, was full of ideas . . . for passionate teamwork!

#448 THE POWER WITHIN—Dawn Flindt
Strongman Joe Rustin had saved Tina's life. He then became her exercise coach and devoted companion—but *not* the lover she longed for. How could she convince Joe to unleash his powerful inner passions?

#449 RAPTURE DEEP—Anne Lacey
When lovely, treacherous Stacey reentered Chris Lorio's life, buried rage surfaced . . . as did memories of rapture in each other's arms. For the long-ago lovers, the past held bitterness, secrets and, somewhere, sweet promise.

#450 DISARRAY—Linda Shaw
In small-town Finley, Arkansas, little went unnoticed—especially not "good girl" Barbara Regent's canceled wedding, compromised reputation and budding romance with a mysterious, untrusted outsider.

AVAILABLE THIS MONTH:

#439 CATCH A FALLING STAR
Brooke Hastings

#440 MORE THAN A MISTRESS
Joan Mary Hart

#441 THE PRIDE OF HIS LIFE
Bevlyn Marshall

#442 LOOK HOMEWARD, LOVE
Pat Warren

#443 HEAT LIGHTNING
Lynda Trent

#444 FOREVER SPRING
Joan Hohl

Silhouette Intimate Moments

THIS MONTH
CHECK IN TO
DODD MEMORIAL HOSPITAL!

Not feeling sick, you say? That's all right, because Dodd Memorial isn't your average hospital. At Dodd Memorial you don't need to be a patient—or even a doctor yourself!—to examine the private lives of the doctors and nurses who spend as much time healing broken hearts as they do healing broken bones.

In UNDER SUSPICION (Intimate Moments #229) intern Allison Schuyler and Chief Resident Cruz Gallego strike sparks from the moment they meet, but they end up with a lot more than love on their minds when someone starts stealing drugs—and Allison becomes the main suspect.

In May look for AFTER MIDNIGHT (Intimate Moments #237) and finish the trilogy in July with HEARTBEATS (Intimate Moments #245).

Author Lucy Hamilton is a former medical librarian whose husband is a doctor. Let her check you in to Dodd Memorial—you won't want to check out!

IM229-1R